Paul's Perfect Princess

A DDLG and ABDL romantic age play love story about an unlikely Daddy Dom finding his perfect baby girl

By Tina Moore

Table of Contents

Chapter 1

Hannah frantically read over her notes in the break room, reviewing them again and again as if she hadn't long ago memorized the information. Claire watched her with amusement as Hannah muttered under her breath from time to time and chewed on her finger anxiously.

"I wouldn't so blatant about that if I were you," Claire chimed in. "Mr. Williams would blow a fuse if he saw you studying on company time." Hannah looked up at her, so focused on the task at hand that it took several moments for the words to register.

"Huh? Oh, I was just going over these notes one last time. My last final is at four o'clock this afternoon and traffic is so bad this time of day. I don't think I'll have time for any last-minute cramming after work, so I'm trying to fit it all in now."

"What are you so worried about anyway? You know all of this by heart. You've done nothing but live, eat, and breathe Marine Biology since I met you. You should be enjoying your upcoming freedom. You're going to ace this test just like you've aced every test since I've known you. So relax a little already. Haven't you ever heard of senioritis?"

"I'll relax once I've graduated," Hannah muttered. Claire looked at her through narrow eyes.

"Is that so? I'll remember that you said that. I know of a couple of really good parties going on next weekend."

"Wait. What? No, I didn't mean it like that. "Claire was always trying to drag her to some party or another, but Hannah always declined. Between work and school, she just didn't have time for any kind of socializing. Even if she did have the time, she hated parties, preferring to get together with small groups of friends rather than the kinds of parties that Claire liked to attend.

Crowds made her nervous, and she could never relax enough to enjoy herself if there were too many people and a bunch of loud noises. Mr. Williams came in and hurriedly made a beeline for the coffee pot. Hannah felt like she had been saved by the bell until she remembered that she was on the clock. She jumped to hide her notes before he noticed them, shoving them awkwardly in her bathing suit. As he turned around and nodded at the girls in greeting, he did a double-take at the strange, crumpled lump under Hannah's suit but only shook his head. Hannah did her best to behave as though nothing was amiss.

"Claire, your tour group, has arrived, you had better get out there." He took a loud slurp of his coffee and leaned against the counter.

"Sure thing, Mr. Williams," she said with a fake cheeriness and left. Hannah hated it when she did that; it was so awkward. She could never tell if Mr. Williams didn't realize that she was being sarcastic or if he just didn't care. Both seemed equally as likely.

"Hey, don't you have a big test today or something?" he asked, loudly slurping on his coffee once again. It was such an annoying habit that set Hannah's teeth on edge.

"My last final. It all comes down to this." She felt her stomach tighten, her nervousness coming back full force. It wasn't the information that was going to be on the final that had her so anxious but rather the finality of it all. Four years of working toward a singular goal, and she was finally within sight of the finish line. All she had to do was try not to fall flat on her face. Right. No problem. She chewed on her lip again, feeling a raw spot starting to form there.

"Well, good luck and try not to get too in your head about it, you don't want to get the yips. Hey, why don't you take off early today since there are no more tour groups scheduled? I expect it will be pretty quiet around here for the rest of the day. If there are any last-minute bookings, Claire can handle it."

"Oh, thank you so much, Mr. Williams!" she

said, a wave of relief washing over her. "I really needed that extra time to study."

"Oh, you'll do fine, you're a smart kid. Now go knock 'em dead." Hannah was so grateful that she hugged the man before rushing off the locker room. She grabbed her bag and slipped on a pair of jean shorts and a t-shirt over her bathing suit, not willing to spare the time it would take to change. She waited until she got to her car before pulling the crumpled notes out of her bathing suit. They were a little damp but still readable. She smoothed them out on the steering wheel, looking them over again before heading to class. In truth, she really did know all of this information front and backward, but going over her notes soothed her nerved. As she tried to crank her car, however, there was only a terrible sound of metal grinding on metal before it went dead again. She tried to turn the engine again, but the grinding sound only got worse, followed by a plume of black smoke that came out from under the hood. So much for her nerves. Hannah cursed and popped the hood, getting out of the car in a huff, despairing that this would happen at such an inconvenient moment. She tried to pry the hood the rest of the way open, but the metal was hot to the touch, and she jerked her hand away with another curse. Tears of pain and frustration sprung to her eyes, and she could feel panic beginning to rise in her throat, feeling at a total loss. Should she call a mechanic first or a cab first? It was so hard to think straight with her heart pounding.

"Whoa, there, pretty lady," she heard a deep voice behind her say. She turned to find the most handsome man she had ever seen approaching her. As he got closer, she recognized him as Paul Peterson: local celebrity, professional surfer, and an all-around popular party guy. Hannah had seen him at the beach pretty frequently, practicing his moves and flirting with the girls that were always flocking around him. He was hard not to notice, classically handsome, charismatic, incredibly fit. He had shiny black hair, brown eyes, and a broad frame. She had never even considered trying to talk to him before. He seemed like he was from another world and she was content to watch him from afar.

"Need a hand?" asked Paul. She instantly felt a jolt of attraction as their eyes met, making her legs feel a bit wobbly all of a sudden. She had only ever seen him from across the beach or on local television. Up close and in person was a whole other ballgame. He looked her up and down appraisingly, then smiled in a way that made it obvious that he liked what he saw, and she could feel her body responding to him despite the stressful situation.

"Um, yeah, I guess I do," she said, feeling a bit dazed. The car trouble suddenly seemed even more annoying because she had to focus on that when she would rather be flirting with this handsome gentleman.

"What seems to be the problem?" he asked. Again, she felt a tingling heat come over her as she stared into his eyes, dumbstruck for a moment. She tore her eyes away from him reluctantly and looked at the smoking wreckage that had been a functioning vehicle just that morning.

"Um, I'm really not sure, it just started doing this just now," she said. The panic came rushing back, and she was sure that he could hear it in her voice. "I don't know a thing about cars, unfortunately, so I really don't have a clue what could be wrong with it."

"Ok, well, don't worry, miss," said Paul, flashing the brightest smile at her that she had ever seen. "It just so happens that I'm friends with the best mechanic in town. I can give him a call if you'd like, ask him to send a wrecker out and take a look at it."

"No," she said, shaking her head. "That's too much. I couldn't ask you to do that."

"You didn't ask," he retorted with a wink. "And neither did I. There is no way that I'm leaving a pretty lady as you stranded here like this." She found herself blushing and annoyed at the same time, a strange combination. The wild roller coaster of emotions had left her feeling on edge.

"So if I weren't pretty, you would leave me stranded here?" she asked, putting her hands on her hips. He laughed, throwing his head back. The sunlight glinted off his shiny black hair, and all trace of annoyance disappeared instantly. How could anyone ever be annoyed at such beauty?

"Of course not," he said, still chuckling. "I just wanted an excuse to let you know that you're pretty."

"Oh," she said, feeling suddenly chagrined. "I don't need you to tell me I'm pretty. I already know that." She said with an unimpressed look. She must have dropped one of her notecards because Paul spotted one of her them being blown away by the wind and chased it down with feline grace and speed.

"Is this yours?" he asked, handing it to her.

"Oh no! I'm going to be so late for my final!" She mentally kicked herself for spending her time flirting with him when she had real problems to deal with.

"When and where is it?" asked Paul.

"It's not far, luckily, and it doesn't start for another couple of hours, but who knows how long it will take to get the wrecker out here! And then I'll have to get a cab! Oh no, I'm really going to be late." Her voice got more and more frantic as she listed off her problems. Paul shook his head and fished his car keys out of his pocket.

"No, you don't need to worry about any of that. You just worry about passing your final. How about I'll trade you my car for yours. Let me take care of your car. You can get mine back to me in a few days."

"But, how will you get around?" she asked reluctantly. She couldn't just take this guy's car, could she? They had only known each other for a couple of minutes.

"I have another one," said Paul shrugging. "I'll take an Uber home and drive my other car until yours is fixed." He pulled a business card out from his wallet. "Text your name to this number. What is your name, by the way?"

"Hannah," she said quietly, taking the card.

"I'm having a party tomorrow night at my place. You should hang out, have a few drinks. It will be fun!" Hannah nodded slowly as they shoved the keys into her hands. He put a hand on the small of her back and started guiding her towards her car. That small, subtly dominant touch set her inner core on fire, and she was suddenly finding it very hard to think.

"Are you sure you want just to give me your car? You just met me. I could be some sleazy dirtbag who's going to take your car and sell it on the black market for all you know." Again, he laughed making Hannah blush even deeper. Surely the idea of her being a criminal wasn't that laughable.

"I am absolutely certain. The only thing I want you worrying about right now is your test. Promise?"

"Ok," she sighed. "I guess that I'm not really in a position to argue." Paul was opening the driver's side door for her and shooing her into the vehicle.

"You'd better get going now. I'll see you tomorrow at the party tomorrow night."

"Ok, I'll see you there." For a moment, she could only watch him and wondered what the heck had just happened before she came back to herself and put the car in drive. She did her best to put his handsome face out of her mind and focus.

Chapter 2

Hannah was already at work when Claire dragged herself in the next morning, looking like hell had warmed over. Hannah had been pouring herself a cup of coffee and after one look at Claire, poured her a cup as well.

"Rough night?" she asked as she slid the cup across the counter. Claire nodded and gratefully took several deep gulps from the mug before coming up for air, giving a big satisfied sigh.

"Yes, I was partying really late last night. Thank you so much for the coffee. I really needed that. Oh hey, how did the test go?" she asked, swatting Hannah playfully on the arm.

"Ugh, I think I did, OK. I second-guessed myself on a lot the answers and spent so long debating if it was right or not that I ran out of time. They won't post my grades for a few days, so I'll just have to wait until then to find out." Hannah's face twisted, thinking about how fraught with anxiety she would be over the next few days. She didn't think it would be possible to concentrate on anything else.

"I still don't get why you're so freaked out. Even if you totally bombed it, which I doubt, there's no way you could fail with such a high GPA, right?"

"Yeah, that's true," Hannah sighed. "But I wouldn't be able to graduate with honors."

"Oh," Claire said, nodding slowly. "I guess that is a pretty big deal. But, hey, what's done is done, and I am sure you did fine. You are by far the smartest person I know. And no matter what happens with this test, you are finally done. Done with school and studying and all-nighters followed by early morning shifts, done with being permanently exhausted. I say that calls for a celebration." Hannah laughed at the coincidence.

"It's funny. You should mention that. You've heard of Paul Peterson, right?" Claire nodded impatiently. Of course, she had, everyone around here knew who he was.

"Well, he's throwing a party this evening at his beach house, and he invited me." Claire nearly choked on her coffee at that revelation.

"What?!" she screeched. "He invited you personally? Why didn't you lead with that? When did you meet him?"

"Yesterday," Hannah confessed. "I had a little car trouble on my way to my test, and he rescued me."

"What, like he helped you change your flat tire? That's so hot. Did he take his shirt off like in the movies?" Claire's enthusiasm was so infectious that Hannah laughed, blushing slightly at the image. Suddenly she wished that he had taken off his shirt.

"No, it was a lot worse than a flat tire. He had to call a wrecker. It was so bad. I was freaking out about being late for my test, and Paul just let me borrow his car." Claire's eyebrows shot up.

"What? He just gave you his car? He must

want you pretty bad."

"What, me? Why would you say that? Maybe he's just a nice guy. He has plenty of money, I'm sure. He's constantly winning surfing championships and getting endorsement deals."

"Rich or not, nice guys don't just go around handing over their cars to strange women that they just met. That dude wants to put it in you."

"Claire!" she gasped. "That's so crass!" Claire just shrugged and grinned, unrepentant.

"The truth is the truth. I might not be as smart as you, but I know men. Snap him up while you can. You are going to the party, right? I know it isn't your usual thing, but you absolutely cannot miss this. How often do rich handsome men invite you over to party with them?"

"Yes, I'm going. I'm supposed to give the car back to him then so I pretty much have to. I'm nervous about going, though. You know how much I hate parties."

"Don't look at it as a party; look at it as a networking opportunity. You're a recent college graduate about to enter the workforce. You need to get out there and meet some of the folks in the community instead of hiding behind a book all the time." Hannah had to admit that Claire had a good point there. She wasn't originally from the island and didn't actually know many people. If she wanted to stay here and get a job, which she did, she would have to get out there and meet someone whose aunt's neighbor or whatever had an in with a local aquarium or conservation group. Hannah had been too busy for an internship, having to spend all of her free time working someplace that could pay, and that meant she was already a step behind most of the other graduates in the marine biology program. She sighed in defeat, knowing it was unavoidable. Claire squealed with delight and did a happy little dance.

"Excellent, what time are you going?"

"It starts at eight."

"Don't you dare show up before nine-thirty. Oh, and you had better wear something slutty." Hannah blushed and crossed her arms over her chest self-consciously.

"I most certainly will not," she said indignantly. "How would that help my chances of getting a job?" Claire scoffed.

"That's not what I'm worried about. You need to get laid, like yesterday." Hannah's blush deepened to her chest, wondering what had brought on such crass language all of a sudden. Claire knew how much she hated that.

"Claire!" she hissed, embarrassed.

"What?!" asked Claire innocently. "I don't think I've ever even heard you mention a date, much less a boyfriend. You need some companionship, the touch of another human being, or I swear to god you're going to pop like a little overworked, undersexed balloon."

"Whatever," muttered Hannah, hoping to drop the conversation before she died of embarrassment. Claire picked up her mug of coffee and headed toward the break room door to start her day. She paused by the door, giving Hannah one last word of advice before she left.

"Slutty," she said pointedly and let the door swing shut behind her.

Chapter 3

Hannah parked Paul's car at the address he had texted her. She may not know much about cars, but this one was obviously much nicer than hers, and she was going to miss having heated seats and windows you didn't have to crank open by hand. There were a bunch of people out on the front lawn, drinking and talking. Hannah didn't see anyone she recognized, but that was to be expected. She went in and did a lap around the house looking for Paul, but she didn't see him yet, so she passed the time admiring the house instead. It was a modern design with lots of light-colored wood and an open airy floor plan. It was the perfect beach house. She reflected as she examined the built-in bookshelves and wondered how much the whole thing cost. To her surprise, the books were a little higher brow than she expected. She felt a pang of guilt at the thought, knowing that she really shouldn't stereotype people. Just because they were surfers didn't mean they weren't perfectly intelligent. Still, she honestly didn't expect to come across an extensive science fiction collection. She saw a book by an author she had been meaning to check but hadn't gotten around to yet. She took one last look around the room for Paul and, when she didn't see him, slipped the book into her bag and went upstairs. There were some empty bedrooms up there, and she picked the one that looked the most like a guest room. She didn't want to violate anyone's privacy. She just wanted a quiet place to read and escape the crowd for a while. She sat in a chair next to a desk, one foot tucked under her, and turned on the desk lamp. Soon, she was completely engrossed in the story and completely lost track of time and what she was supposed to be doing. Some time into the third chapter, she heard the door creak open and looked up to see Paul.

"Oh, hello!" he said good-naturedly, looking

surprised yet very happy to see her. "Did you get lost?"

"Not exactly," Hannah said shyly. "I just wanted to find a quiet spot, and it didn't seem like anyone was using this room at the moment. Sorry if I bothered something."

"You're not bothering a thing, pretty lady. What book do you have there?" He looked a little closer and nodded approvingly. "A woman of refined tastes, I see. That is one of my personal favorites." Paul was wearing a pair of distressed khakis and a green button-up that complimented his chocolate eyes and dark features perfectly. It gave him a slightly more refined air, a side of him she had no idea existed.

"You know you look a lot different when you're not on the beach," she said.

"Let me guess. You almost didn't recognize me with my shirt on?" She blushed which only made him laugh harder. It was an infectious laugh, and Hannah found herself smiling despite her faux pas.

"I guess you get that a lot, huh?" she asked, hoping that at least she wasn't the only one.

"Oh, all the time. It's kind of nice actually, almost like having a secret identity. Shirtless Surfer Man by day and boring old Paul by night."

"I've only just met you, but it's hard to imagine you being boring." It came out of her mouth before she even realized how flirty is sounded. "I mean, your book collection alone is fascinating." Somehow that last part sounded even more flirty. She tried not to blush again but was sure that she was failing.

"Why, thank you. You can take that home with you if you like. Just bring it back by anytime when you're finished." He winked at her when he said that last part and Hannah wondered if he was flirting back or just being friendly. She had never been able to tell the difference until they were directly asking her out.

"You're so kind. Oh, that reminds me, here are your keys back. I can't thank you enough for letting me borrow it." He only shook his head and waved them away.

"I'm afraid your car won't be ready for a couple more days. My mechanic friend says he will have to order a part from the mainland, and you know how long that can take. You hold on to those for a few more days. Why are you up here all alone?" he asked abruptly, changing the subject, interrupting her objections before she could give them.

"Oh, I just got a little overwhelmed by the crowd. I don't know anyone, and parties make me nervous." She cringed inside, wondering what kind of boring wallflower she was sounding like to this handsome, charming, social butterfly.

"To tell you the truth," he leaned in conspiratorially. "Parties make me nervous too. I was actually slipping up here to escape the crowd as well. It's getting kind of crazy down there." She gave him a skeptical look, wondering if he was only humoring her.

"But this is your party. Why would you throw a party if they make you nervous?"

"It's good for business," he shrugged and walked over the window, looking out at the partygoers on the front yard. "Most endorsement deals happen because of who you know rather than what you can do. I'm relatively unknown in the sport at the moment, so I have to hustle a little harder. Besides, I know most of these people, some of them really well. That helps a lot. Would you like me to introduce you to some nice folks? It might make you feel a little less nervous." She bit her lip, wanting to stay in this nice quiet room with this nice handsome man, but she knew that she should suck it up and go make some new friends.

"Tell you what. We'll make the rounds for ten minutes. Then we can come back up here and take another breather. How does that sound?"

"Really? That's so sweet. Okay, yeah, let's do it." He motioned toward the door, indicating that she should go first. As she walked by, he put his hand on the small of her back, guiding her through the door as he held it open for her. She felt her heart fluttering at the romantic gesture. If was even meant to be romantic. Maybe he was just nice. Again, the old conundrum. They went downstairs, and Paul pulled a few people to the side to make introductions. She found herself answering the same questions over and over again. What do you do? Are you seeing anyone? Isn't Paul totally awesome? By the end of the ten minutes, her head was swimming. She didn't know how she was ever going to remember any of those names, and she was sure she would remember less than half of the faces. She felt Paul's hand on the small of her back again, leading her towards the stairs, and she let him lead her, grateful for the break.

"Well, that was a good round, I think," he said once they were back in their hiding spot. "We can go back down again later if you want. For now, I'd like to further make your acquaintance if I may." She noticed that he was looking at her expectantly. She suddenly felt a little overwhelmed by the attention. Such a handsome, kind man looking at her as though she were a tasty snack, it was almost too much.

"Well, sure, but I think you'll find that I'm rather boring." Paul shook his head. "I don't believe that for a second. Why would you say that?"

"All I do is work and study."

"What do you study?" asked Paul.

"I study Marine Biology, or at least I did. I took my last test today, and I'll graduate in a couple of weeks."

"Wow, that's amazing," said Paul. "It must have been really difficult to put yourself through school like that. That's quite an accomplishment. Although if you work down at the marina, I'm surprised I haven't seen you before yesterday. I'm there all the time."

"I've seen you," she shrugged. "But, there's usually a bit of a crowd around you."

"And you hate crowds," Paul laughed. "Still, I feel like I would have noticed you, even across a crowded beach. You're a very lovely woman,

Hannah." Hannah blushed yet again. She got the uncanny feeling that he was undressing her with his eyes, and she suddenly didn't know where to look or what to do with her hands. She tried to change the subject.

"Well, I'll be down there even more now that I'm done with school. I'll be doing dolphin tours full time now, I suppose."

"You don't have another job lined up yet? One closer to your field, I mean." She sighed and bit her lip before answering, not wanting to load this kind gentleman down with her sob story.

"No, I've put in a few applications but no callbacks yet. They give preference to people with internship experience, and I couldn't afford that. I just have to hope that they get desperate, and I get lucky." He looked thoughtful for a moment.

"If you'd like, I can make some inquiries around town. I know lots of folks in town. Surely some of them are looking for a capable yet beautiful Marine Biologist." Hannah's face lit up. She couldn't believe it. She had suddenly gone from having no leads to having the most influential person in town, offering his help. She wondered vaguely which lucky star she had to thank for this small miracle.

"Really, you would do that for me?" she gushed.

"Of course I would," said Paul. "I would love to help you." She was glowing from within, feeling very lucky indeed to have made such a wonderful friend. It was flattering, having the full attention of a man who was constantly surrounded by beautiful women. That he was willing to go so far out of his way for her was incredibly touching.

"As a matter of fact, I'm having another event the day after tomorrow, a surfing demo. Would you like to come? It probably won't be as crowded as the party tonight was."

"Ok," she said, trying to sound casual when really she was eager for a chance to see him again. "Yeah, I can try to make that. What time?"

"It starts at four," said Paul. "But if you can get there early, you can hang out with me in the 'green room' which in reality is really just a tent with a cooler. You in?"

"Yeah, I'll see if I can get off work a couple of hours early." He grinned, suddenly looking very proud of himself.

"Well, alright then, sounds like a date," said Paul, looking as happy as a clam. Hannah was certain that he didn't mean it the way that it sounded, but she blushed anyway. He wouldn't be interested in someone like her, would he? He did seem like he was flirting with her, but she couldn't see why he would like someone like her.

"Well, I guess I'd better take off," she said, beginning to feel the effects of the late hour and a long stressful week. He looked incredibly disappointed.

"So soon?" asked Paul, standing up from the desk. "Why don't you stay a bit longer? I could go get us some drinks." Hannah was tempted but only shook her head.

"No, it's getting pretty late for my tastes, to be honest, I'm somewhat of an early bird. And I have work again tomorrow."

"Well, alright, if you must you must," said Paul. He held out his hand for her to shake. As she took it, it was warm and engulfed her hand like she imagined a bear's paw would. Now that he was standing, she noticed how much taller than her he was, how he loomed over her, dominant energy coming off of him like waves. He shook her hand a couple of times, then raised it to his lips to kiss her knuckle reverently. He looked at her and winked before dropping her hand. "It was very nice to see you again, Hannah. I hope that we see each other again soon."

"Thank you," she said breathlessly. "I hope that we do, too. Thank you for a lovely evening. This is by far the best party I've ever been to." They both laughed and waved at one another as she edged her way reluctantly towards the door. She secretly wished that she could stay here for the rest of the night but was also afraid that she would blow it if she did. When she opened the door, the din of the party invaded their little sanctuary, breaking the magic that it seemed to hold. With one last wave over her shoulder, she left.

***

Paul tossed and turned all night, scarcely able to rid himself of the thoughts of Hannah that plagued even his dreams. How he longed to spread those perfect thighs and slide himself inside of her, to feel her squirm and moan beneath him, calling him Daddy as she wrapped herself around him and begged for more. Hannah was kind, smart, beautiful, and every part of him was on fire at the thought of her, and he had to possess her completely.

She's probably not a little, Paul warned himself. *She probably doesn't even know what it means. Don't get your hopes up.* Still, there was something about her that made him hopeful. Being a Daddy was hard sometimes. He longed for a real relationship, a baby girl that he could call his very own, but all of the women he'd dated were varying levels of disinterested or disgusted by his affinity. Paul sighed heavily, wishing he could dress Hannah up in pretty dresses, buy her all the toys her heart desired, and snuggle up next to her every night. Snuggling wasn't all he dreamed of doing to her. What he wouldn't give to hear her call him Daddy as he fucked her. The thought was too much, and he grasped his hard cock, desperate for relief. He stroked his cock feverishly, imagining it was Hannah's delicate pink lips wrapped around his hardness instead of his own hand. In his mind's eye, her cheeks were flushed pink after cumming like a good girl so many times on his cock that they both had lost count. Her eyes fluttered closed as she gripped his buttocks and bucked her hips against his, milking him with her tight little cunt.

"Cum for me, Daddy," she would whisper, and he would empty his load so deep inside of her. He grunted and soiled his sheets, cumming with a shuddering groan. He kicked his wet sheets to the floor, but it wasn't enough to relieve the tension.

Eventually, he fell into a fitful sleep, still whispering Hannah's name.

Chapter 4

Hannah put extra time into her hair and makeup the day of the demo, knowing that she was going to be seeing her new favorite guy. She picked out her cutest outfit, a dress that was tight enough to show off her curves but also concealed her diaper. She almost hadn't worn it, but she figured that if anything romantic did happen with Paul, she could just excuse herself to the bathroom and take it off. She had gotten very good at hiding this part of her life from romantic partners over the years. Secretly, she dreamed of finding a Daddy of her very own someday, someone to pamper her and take care of her, but for now she was content to keep her secret. Wearing a diaper soothed her nerves, and she was every bit as nervous as she was excited. Paul had been texting her all day, telling her how excited he was to see her, too. She followed his directions and found the place easily enough. It took her a few minutes of trying to calm the butterflies in her stomach before she could go in, however. Finally, she calmed herself enough to enter the tent. It was actually very nice inside, much more than "just a tent with a cooler" as he had so humbly put it. There was a DJ and a full bar, as well as a dozen or more people mingling around. The tent was large enough that it didn't seem at all crowded, something that put her a little more at ease. Paul spotted her around the same time, and she noticed that when he saw her, his face lit up. He quickly disentangled himself from his current conversation with a couple of guys in suits and rushed right over to her. He was in his swim trunks already, but blessedly he still had his t-shirt on. She was fairly certain that her head would literally explode if he came at her shirtless. It seemed as though Claire was right about her needing to get laid.

"Glad you could make it," he said slyly. The gleam in his chocolatey brown eyes told her that he was very glad indeed. The way he looked at her, raw hunger on his face, made her burn for him.

"Thank you for inviting me," she said, hoping that she wasn't blushing. "This is really great."

"Would you like a drink?" he asked.

"Yeah, a drink sounds really nice," she said. She was hoping that a little bit of liquid courage would loosen her up a bit. As he led her toward the bar, Paul put a hand on the small of her back, subtly maneuvering her. The gesture made her sweat a little, her heart suddenly beating faster. She ordered a beer, and he waved away her card, telling the bartender to put it on his tab.

"Are you kidding? You don't pay for anything when you're with me," he said with a wink and handed her the beer. She blushed and tried to hide it by taking a sip of the foamy beer.

"Thanks, that's really nice," she said once she had recovered a few her wits.

"Would you like me to introduce you around the room?" asked Paul, leaning in close to ask. The feel of his breath on her neck had her feeling a bit woozy.

"Maybe in a minute," she said, suddenly feeling like she might need to sit down. "But don't let me hold you back, you go ahead and mingle if you need to." He shook his head.

"Oh no, I'm not leaving your side until the event starts. Can't have some other guy come and snap you up now, can I?" She giggled at the unlikely though and sipped her beer again, trying to regain her composure. She didn't think there was a single man in the universe who could tear her away from Paul at that moment.

"Oh, that reminds me," Paul said. "You left that book behind the other night. You were only three chapters in, just wait until chapter eight, you won't believe it!"

"You've read it?"

"Of course! I've read the whole series dozens of times."

"That's really cool. Thanks for the reminder, I've been meaning to read more lately, especially now that I have more free time."

"Speaking of which, what are you doing after this?" asked Paul.

"Nothing. My boss gave me the whole day off work, so I'm totally free." She cringed inwardly, hoping that she didn't sound too overeager.

"Good," he said, a bit lower so no one would overhear. "I want to take you somewhere private after this." He was giving her that look again like he was undressing her with their eyes. She felt hot all over her body under his gaze.

"Where do you want to go?" It didn't really matter to her where they went. She had a feeling that she would follow him anywhere. Before he could answer, a very drunk guy in a black t-shirt came over and started gushing about what a big fan he was. Paul handled him graciously, signing autographs for him and taking selfies with him. The guy eventually went away happy, presumably to go get even drunker.

"Sorry about that," said Paul. "Look, I have to go get ready for this thing now, but it shouldn't take too long. Then I have a quick interview, but I'll do my best to speed through it. Would you mind waiting around for a while? It'll be worth it, I promise."

"Yeah, of course, I'll stick around. I'm really excited about seeing you surf finally. Everyone says you are the best."

"Why, thank you," he grinned. "Just stick to the tent. For now, no one should bother you here. They'll announce when I'm about to go out. Think you'll be OK on your own for a while?"

"Yeah, of course. I'll just hang here, and you can text me when you're done."

"OK, cool. I'll see you soon." He kissed her hand again before disappearing.

Chapter 5

The surfing demo was very interesting to watch. Paul did tricks and flips that Hannah had never even heard of before. Not that she knew much about surfing in the first place. She was a strong swimmer and boogie boarder but had never had the time or inclination to learn how to surf. Everyone in the crowd oohed and ahhed as he did his tricks, and Hannah felt very proud of her new friend. It was clear to her that he took his craft very seriously, something that only made him more attractive to her.

As she watched him in action, she pondered on their newfound friendship. There was an undeniable sexual chemistry between them, something that she found exciting but also confusing. Maybe she was misreading things, and what she had thought was flirtatious behavior was really just kindness. Maybe he just wanted to be friends. She hoped not, though, she realized as she watched his tanned muscular body move under the afternoon sun. Watching him being so physical made her want to get physical with him as well and not on a surfboard. It had been a while since she had met anyone that she was attracted to, but it was undeniable the way that this man-made her feel. It was intoxicating to imagine his hands on her, his lips kissing her neck and breasts. She even indulged herself by imagining calling him "Daddy" in her fantasy, hearing him whisper "baby girl" before he pulled her close for a passionate kiss.

As she was lost in her reverie, someone snatched her purse and ran off with it into the crowd. She snapped herself back to reality and called after the thief, crying out for someone to stop him, but he was gone in a flash before anyone could react. She tried combing through the crown but to no avail.

As she looked around at the sea of strange faces, she began to realize how screwed she actually was. Everything that she needed was in that bag.

She had been so concerned with looking cute that she had worn an outfit with no pockets. That meant her wallet, her cellphone, Paul's car keys, everything was now gone. As tears began to spring to her eyes, she noticed that people were beginning to look at her strangely which only made her more upset. She was sure that she looked like a crazy person, with panicked eyes and smeared mascara. She started pushing her way to the back of the crowd, wanting to get away and find a quiet place to think. She had no idea how she was going to get a hold of Paul or how she was going to get home. Once she did, how would she ever be able to tell Paul that she had lost his car keys after he had trusted her with them? Was their blossoming friendship already over before it had a chance to really begin? That last thought was so upsetting to her that her eyes were suddenly full of tears, completely blurring her vision. The crowd was beginning to disperse, and people were bumping into her, pushing her first in one direction and then the next. She was so upset and overwhelmed that before she realized it, she was on a strange part of the beach, with no idea which direction she had gone or how to get back. She fantasized about Paul swooping in to rescue her and holding her safely in his big, strong arms.

Stop being a stupid baby. She scolded herself. She wiped her eyes, trying to pull herself together. She had to formulate a plan, and for that, she had to sit and think. To calm herself down. She found a place in the sand to sit for a minute and closed her eyes, doing some deep breathing exercises that she had learned her freshman year. Any time she was feeling overwhelmed or stressed out she would practice this deep breathing and it made everything just a little bit easier to handle. Finally, after a few minutes, she felt clear-headed enough to figure out a solution to her problem. She started by asking random passersby if they knew which direction the tent was, but none of them knew what she was talking about. Instead, she started asking about the surfing demo, but even that took several tries before someone could point her in the right direction. She trudged through the sand, her cute sandals now cutting into her feet with every step. All she really wanted to do was to curl up somewhere dark and quiet and go to sleep, but she kept going, telling herself again that now was not the time to be a big pouty baby. There would be time for that later. She giggled at her own unfunny joke, despite her dire circumstances, and that made her feel a little better. She thought that she was starting to recognize her surroundings. Again, she felt a small ray of hope. Just as she was starting to feel like she might be ok again, the strap on her sandals broke, and she fell face-first into the sand. She heard a couple of snickers from the people around her, but one kind soul reached down to help her up.

"Oh dear," said the lady, who looked like a kindly grandmother. "You seem to have bumped your nose there. Here, have a tissue." The elderly lady fished in her bag for a crumpled up napkin, which Hannah took gratefully. The lady patted her hand sympathetically and waddled off. As Hannah dabbed at her nose, she saw that there was indeed blood on the tissue. At the sight of it, her knees grew weak, and she got very dizzy. She could feel herself sinking back down into the sand, a bit more gradually this time, hitting the sand with her knees first before everything went black.

***

When she woke up, Paul was kneeling over her, his handsome face scrunched up with concern. She had a disoriented moment where she wondered why he was in her bedroom. Then she remembered they were at the beach. She had been trying to find him, lost and upset. Then she remembered seeing the blood and fainting. Her head was aching, and she felt like an idiot lying in the sand like that. Frantically, she pulled her skirt down, praying that no one had seen her diaper as she lay sprawled out and unconscious. As she tried to sit up, however, a pair of strong hands was gently pushing her back down.

"Oh no you don't," said Paul. "You don't move a muscle until the EMTs can take a look at you." She groaned and covered her face in humiliation.

"No, please tell me you didn't call an ambulance. I only fainted, I'm fine."

"I called an ambulance and the cops," he replied. "When I tried to Facetime you, some guy answered and tried to extort money from me in exchange for your phone back. I figured that you must have been mugged or something, and I've been looking for you ever since. How long have you been lying out here like this?"

"I'm not sure, exactly. After I got mugged, I got lost. Then, my sandal broke, and my nose was bleeding, and I've never been good with blood." She trailed off, not wanting to cry in front of Paul.

"There, there little one," said Paul. "Don't cry. It's all my fault. I never should have left you alone like that. It will never happen again, I promise. I never dreamed that something like this could happen, can you ever forgive me?"

"Forgive you? What are you talking about? This wasn't your fault."

"Oh yes, it was," said Paul grimly. "I wasn't there to protect you. I didn't even leave you with a security guard. I should have known better."

"Paul,' she sighed, dreading telling him this next part. "I don't think you understand. They got your keys." Paul only laughed and shook his head at that, making Hannah squint at him in confusion.

"Good, that will only make it easier for the cops to find him. I always put a tracker in my key fobs because I lose them so frequently. Unless he's smart and ditches the fob. But don't you worry, I'll get your credit cards and I.D.s back from that guy, one way or another. You just leave it all up to me." She had no idea what to say in response to his unfaltering sweetness, but she was relieved of that burden when two EMTs pushed their way through the small crowd that had formed around them. They checked her out briefly, looking at her nose and pupils in particular. Eventually, they declared her to be in good health, saying that she was fine for now but that she should take it easy over the next couple of days. Once the EMTs were gone, Paul finally let her sit up. Now that it seemed that the show was over, the small crowd began to shuffle off as well.

"We need to get you off to bed right away," said Paul. He helped her up, handling her as delicately as possible as though she were made of glass. It was definitely touching but also a little embarrassing. As she put her arm through his to stabilize herself, she noticed that he had her broken sandal in his hand, and she almost started crying again, this time from gratitude.

"I really can't thank you enough. I honestly don't know what I'd do without you."

"That's enough of that, now," Paul said gently. "There is no point wondering what you'd do without me because you won't ever be without me again. Not if I have anything to say about it." She felt a flutter in her heart when he said that, feeling like the luckiest girl in the world to have him in her life. He had already done so much for her, made her feel so special. She leaned into Paul's warmth, taking comfort in his strength. He helped her get into the car and gave her back her broken sandal, but upon closer inspection, it didn't look salvageable. That's what happened when you bought cheap sandals, she supposed. Hannah gave him directions to her house, and they arrived there shortly. Once inside, he insisted that she sit down on the couch as he brought her blankets, books, and a cup of tea. Paul even threatened to make her some soup, but she declined, saying that she just wanted to rest for a while. Once she got him to settle, it actually turned out to be a lovely evening despite all the chaos from earlier. She changed out of the uncomfortable dress and put on some cute but comfy loungewear. The police called Paul to report that they had found the key fob ditched along with her purse and most of her IDs. She would have to cancel her credit cards, which were still missing and get a new phone, but at least she wouldn't have to go to the DMV.

Hannah would take the victory, even if it was a

small one. They streamed some movies and opened a bottle of wine to celebrate. He graciously let Hannah pick out her favorite movies. As they watched Dirty Dancing, Hannah snuck looks at her handsome guest when he wasn't looking, reflecting on what Paul had said earlier about how she would never have to be without him again. Now, she wondered what exactly he meant by that. She didn't want to get her hopes up, but she felt safe being cautiously optimistic as he snuggled in close to her. As they made their way through the first bottle of wine and then opened the second, she couldn't stop thinking about how he had looked out there on the waves, so graceful and assured of himself. He was a magnificent athlete, something that she was sure the result of many hours of practice. That sort of dedication was a very attractive quality to her. She couldn't help but wonder if that kind of stamina extended to the bedroom as well. As the credits began to roll on the movie, she noticed Paul looking at her with a very serious expression on his face.

"Can I ask you a question," he asked. She was almost sure that she detected a hint of nervousness in his voice, something she had never heard from him before. He usually seemed so confident.

"Of course you can," she said.

"I couldn't help but noticing that when you were lying in the sand earlier today, well, I could see your diaper." Her heart sank as she realized that her worst fears had come true. He knew her secret.

"I don't want to pressure you or anything," he continued. "You can tell me to mind my own business if you want. I was just kind of curious." She took a deep breath and decided that she didn't want to hide who she was anymore. He may not like it, but now that he knew, it almost felt like a relief.

"I just like wearing diapers sometimes. I know it's a little weird, but it makes me happy. It's like it calms me down or something." As the words came out, she felt her face get hot, and she looked down at her lap, avoiding his gaze. When she did peek up at him to gauge his reaction, she was surprised to see that he was grinning.

"You're a little. I was hoping that you were."

"You were?!" She had never heard anyone else speak of littles outside of the internet, and she'd always assumed that the odds were way too low ever to meet anyone in real life who shared her preferences.

"I was," he nodded. "You see, I'm a Daddy Dom, so I was secretly wishing that you were the little I've been looking for, I was just too nervous to say anything. I've had many a girl end our association after I've confessed that little tidbit."

"I've never told anyone," she said quietly. "I've always been afraid that they'd have exactly that reaction. You're so brave for telling them the truth. I'm sorry that they reacted that way."

"You're the brave one," he said. "I was too nervous to tell you, but now I don't have too." They beamed at one another, and Hannah felt a rush of joy at his praise. The joy was quickly replaced with a nervous awkwardness. Now that they knew that had that in common, where did that leave them? It might not mean anything. She tried to remind herself. It all just seemed too good to be true.

"Do you want to put another movie on, or are you ready to call it a night?" asked Paul. As he looked at her hopefully, she put those thoughts out of her mind. While she didn't want to get her hopes up, she also wanted to remain open to the possibilities.

"Yeah, I'm up for another. Let's watch Tootsie!" she said enthusiastically.

"Tootsie it is, then," said Paul and started the movie. As they settled back onto the couch, he took her hand in his. She looked at him in surprise, but he only smiled at her. It felt so warm and safe to be snuggled up so close to him on the couch, so right having his hands on her. Some part of her brain wanted to define what was happening, but she did her best not to listen to that part of herself and just enjoyed the moment. Paul poured her another glass of wine, handing it to her with a squeeze of her hand. She sipped it happily and passed it back to him, the two of them sharing one cup. Once the glass was empty, they snuggled together on the couch, a tangle of limbs and warm bodies. She closed her eyes, savoring the moment. It was both arousing and calming at the same time, and she wanted the evening to last forever.

Chapter 6

They must have fallen asleep like that because when Hannah awoke again, it was light outside. Paul was still asleep, and she was trapped under him, with Paul's head on her chest and his arms wrapped tightly around her waist. As much as she was loathe to break the moment, she really had to use the bathroom. Despite her best efforts to disentangle herself without waking him, Paul began to stir.

"Mmm, mornin' beautiful," he muttered as he opened his eyes blearily. "I didn't realize that we slept here." He rubbed his neck as if the night on the couch had left him feeling worse for wear.

"I guess it's a good thing," he said, stretching his arms. "Otherwise, you'd have no way of getting to work today. What time do you have to be in today?"

"Oh, not for a few more hours. We don't open until the afternoon."

"Great!" said Paul. "We have enough time for me to make waffles."

"You cook?" she asked, somewhat taken aback. This man was full of constant surprises. "That's so funny. I love to cook too. Come on. I'll show you where everything is." She gave him a brief tour of the kitchen before excusing herself to the lady's room. When she got back, Paul was in full chef mode. He had even dug out some chocolate chips from the cabinet and mixed them into the batter. He insisted that she sit down at the table and not lift a finger while he put on a pot of coffee. She sat and watched indulgently as he got breakfast ready. If she had a million wishes, she didn't think she could have ended up with a more perfect guy.

"So, where were you going to take me yesterday?" she asked.

"No spoilers," said Paul. "I'm still taking you. What time do you get off today?"

"Not that late, around six, usually. Sometimes I'll get lucky, and there won't be anyone signed up for that last tour, but things are just starting to get busy for the summer, so that probably won't happen."

"Well, leave your bathing suit on when you get off," said Paul. "And that's the only hint you get." She grinned and sipped her coffee coyly.

"Alright, then. I'm looking forward to it," she said.

***

He dropped her off after a delicious breakfast. The day at work seemed to drag on, doubly so because it was Claire's day off, and she couldn't even gossip about the events that her so giddy. She could only watch the clock anxiously and wonder about the surprise they would have for her at the end of her shift. All day, the only thing she could think about was how she had finally found a real-life Daddy. And what's more, she really liked him. Thoughts of diaper changes and spankings danced in her head. She wouldn't have to hide who she was around him. Just that simple fact alone had her practically walking on air. Finally, it was time to clock out. Paul was already waiting for her in his car when she came outside. No matter how she pleaded or begged, he still would not tell her where they were going.

"You're just going to have to live with the suspense," he teased. She pretended to pout, but Paul put his hand on her knee, and she couldn't suppress her grin. At that moment, she felt so happy, with the wind in her hair and the best companion that anyone could ask for. They drove out of the city and out past the suburbs. Soon they were in a part of the island that Hannah had never been to before. It was very rural, and they only passed houses and gas stations. Eventually, they turned down a driveway and came to a gate. Paul punched in a code on the keypad, and they were in. The driveway ended onto a private beach. It was stunningly beautiful. The sand was the purest she had ever seen, almost white as the evening sun bounced off it. The water was a stunning blue-green, clear, and pure. There was not a living soul around them. They had the whole place to themselves. Hannah had never felt so free.

"This is amazing!" she said, looking around in wonder. She shed her shorts and t-shirt, eager to get into the water right away.

"I thought that you of all people would appreciate this," he said, taking her hand and leading her toward the shoreline. She kicked off her flip flops, letting the cool sand kiss her bare feet. The two of them ran into the surf, letting the waves break over their bodies. They dove under and swam far from the shore before finally coming up for air. They laughed as they surfaced, exhilarated by one another, and their shared love of the sea.

"You're a very strong swimmer," said Paul. She noticed that he was still gripping her hand. He suddenly dropped her hand, opting instead to wrap one arm around her waist, pulling her close to him. Paul was nearly facing her, close enough that he could kiss her, a thought that left Hannah breathless. He placed a small soft kiss on the curve of her neck. The brush of his lips sent a jolt of electricity all through her. She gasped slightly as Paul's arms tightened around her waist, and he placed a kiss on the other side of her neck as well. She was flooded with so many sensations and emotions that she felt absolutely overwhelmed. Paul continued his soft kisses on her neck as he began to run his hands over her waist and hips. A wave of arousal, stronger than any she had ever experienced before, took her over as he kissed and caressed her body. She closed her eyes to savor the sensations. He claimed her lips with his, salty, and passionate, and she ran her fingers through his hair. She was so adrift in the pleasure that she would have certainly slipped below the surface if she didn't have a strong man holding her afloat. His tongue was suddenly pushing into her mouth with an eagerness to taste her. She moaned into his open mouth and grabbed at his shoulders to bring him closer. She could feel his erection pressing against her, igniting her desire further.

"Let's go back ashore," she murmured, wanting to be on solid ground so that she could explore him the same way he was exploring her. He took her hands and they both dove under the waves again, gliding under the water back toward the shore. Once their feet could touch the bottom, he was all over again, only this time, her hands were free to roam over his firm, muscled bodies, as she had been longing to do for days. The waves crashed over them as they explored one another with lips, tongues, and hands. He pulled aside her bathing suit, delving his fingers into her aching center, seeking out her most sensitive spot. As he pleasured her, he pulled her straps down to release her ample breasts so that he could claim her nipples with his mouth, kissing and licking them so lovingly. She let herself go completely, leaning her head back as her moans echoed down the empty beach. She could feel the pleasure building, working toward a crescendo. Her hands reached out blindly, looking for something to grab or hold onto. Paul took her hands in his, holding them as he continued to kiss her neck and breasts. His fingers between her legs felt like pure heaven, and as much as she wanted to make this perfect moment last, she couldn't hold back anymore. As the ecstasy broke over her, she cried out and gripped Paul's hand as her body shook. As she came back to herself, sated and content, she wanted to return the pleasure that she had just received. She released Paul's hands and sought out the hardness within his swim trunks. He gave a shuddering gasp as she slipped her hand down past the elastic and gripped him firmly. She stroked him lovingly as their tongues dancing together. Paul quickly gave in to his release. He grabbed her face, kissing her deeply and passionately as she swallowed his moans. He didn't let her come up for air until the last shudder had left his body and his breath began to slow.

He's so perfect. She thought as they clung to each other in the surf and sand. After a few minutes, they made their way slowly further away from the shoreline, collapsing in a heap on the sand, still breathless and giddy. They snuggled close together, his arms encircling her in a tight hug. As she gazed up at the stars that were just barely starting to become visible, she felt like thanking them. They lay like that for so long, reluctant to move lest it would break the magic spell of their happiness, that it was fully dark by the time they began to stir. Reluctantly, they got up, brushing the sand from their bodies and hair. On the way back into town, Hannah stared dreamily out of the window before closing her eyes with a smile on her face and the wind in her hair.

Chapter 7

They went back to Paul's so that she would be able to pick up his other car. He had picked up another fob and retrieved it from the beach while she was at work. The latest update on hers was that the part was in; it was just a matter of waiting for the labor to be finished. When she asked about the expense, he only waved away the question.

"Don't worry about it," Paul said, winking at her. "I already told you, you don't pay for anything when you're with me." He pressed the keys into her hand and kissed her on her forehead. She wanted to protest that it was too much, too extravagant, but then she thought about how many shifts at the marina it would take to pay off such a high mechanic bill and about the student loan payments that she was going to have to start paying soon. And that would be on top of the credit card payments she already struggled to keep up with. If she didn't get a job in her field soon, there would be no way for her to keep up with all of that.

"Well, if you're sure," she said, an edge of uncertainty in her voice.

"Never been surer of anything," said Paul, taking her hand reassuringly. "He's going to cut me a deal since we're friends, and what little bit of cash it will cost will be my graduation present to you." She smiled at that, suddenly feeling much better.

"I suppose I do deserve a graduation present, don't I?" she said playfully, giving him a kiss on the cheek. "Well, I'd better get back home. It's been a really lovely evening, thank you."

"You don't want to stay?" he asked, placing a gentle kiss on the nape of her neck like a little added incentive. "I promise not to keep you up too late." As he pressed his body against hers, Hannah had a suspicion that they would be up very late indeed but found that she didn't mind one bit. He ran his fingertips up and down her back as he kissed and nuzzled her neck and she felt herself turn to putty in his hands. Feeling emboldened, she suddenly grabbed him by his firm buttocks and pulled him closer so that his erection was pressing against her. Her body cried out with a burning need to have him inside of her. He groaned at the intimate contact, and his hot breath against her neck made her ache for him all the more.

"Oh Daddy," she whispered on instinct. At the sound of it, Paul suddenly became fierce, grabbing her by the face to pull her in for a passionate, demanding kiss while at the same time pushing her against the door of his home so that she was trapped between him and the unyielding wood door. She had dreamed for so long of being handled exactly in such a manner but had never experienced it until now. It was everything she had imagined it would be as she felt a clenching heat at her core. As he growled into her mouth, biting her lip and pressing his hard cock against her, she melted into him, wanting him to possess her completely. He began fumbling with the lock as they kissed, not wanting to tear himself away from her even for a second. As he flung the door open, she wrapped her arms around his neck. He hoisted her by the ass, lifting her into his arms, and she wrapped her legs around him as well. He kicked the door closed and began carrying her upstairs, exploring her mouth with his tongue the entire way. He put her down again as they entered his bedroom. Paul got on the bed and looked at her up and down, his eyes hungrily taking in her every feature.

"Strip," said Paul, his voice suddenly taking on an authoritativeness that her body responded to instantly. "I want to see my baby girl." She smiled bashfully, taking off the t-shirt she had on over her bathing suit slowly as his eyes tracked her every movement. Paul began to undo his belt, never taking his eyes off of her as he did so. She slid off her shorts, letting them fall to the floor, leaving her only in her bathing suit. It wasn't the sexiest of lingerie, admittedly, but you would never know that based on the way Paul was looking at her.

"You're so beautiful, little one," Paul said, making her blush deeply. No one had ever looked at her so intensely before, and it filled her with a hungry desire. She ran her hands slowly over her stomach before peeling the top of her suit down. Judging from the sharp inhale from Paul, he liked what he saw.

"Fuck, your tits are so perfect," Paul growled, his voice now thick and velvety with lust. "Everything about you is absolutely perfect." Knowing that she was having such an effect as he watched her, that he was so aroused by her was such an aphrodisiac.

"Now take the rest of it off, right now," he commanded. Hannah gasped as her core clenched with desire, and she hurriedly obeyed, eager to give him whatever he asked for. She was thoroughly intoxicated by his domination over her. Her pussy was dripping wet already, even though he had barely touched her. As she peeled the suit the rest of the way down and proudly displayed herself for him, she heard Paul growl "good girl" and she was filled with glowing pride.

"You're mine now, princess," Paul's voice was hypnotic, commanding. "Every part of you, every inch of you now belongs to me. Do you understand me?"

"Yes." Hannah felt breathless, standing before him, vulnerable and completely naked. Her body yearned for him more powerfully than she ever thought was possible. The raw hunger on his face made her tremble, longing to be consumed by him.

"Say it," said Paul gruffly, his usually sweet voice turned rough with lust. Her body ached for them, and she felt like she was completely under their spell.

"I am yours, every inch of me belongs to you." She could feel herself growing even more excited as she said the words, feeling the weight of what she was promising. Paul was beginning to rub himself over his pants, making the outline of his erection more visible. Hannah licked her lips, unable to take her eyes off of it.

"That's right. Fuck, you are so perfect. Come here right now." She joined him on the bed, kneeling before him. His hands were all over her, caressing her adoringly yet urgently. She let her eyes close as his touches grew bolder, exploring the curve of her hips, her generous breasts, and the heat between her legs. Passionate energy radiated from him, leaving her feeling breathless. He pulled her down onto the bed, and she reclined against the pillows as he began to cover her naked flesh with kisses. She returned his caresses, kissing him with all of the fiery need that she felt inside. The orgasm he had given her earlier had did very little to sate her hunger for him. As Paul took her nipple in his mouth, she moaned loudly, and it was as if she were galvanized by him. Her electric desire made her impatient, and she took his hand, guiding it to the very center of her desire. His mouth trailed behind his hand, making her shiver with delight. He found her clit with his soft tongue as he slipped his finger inside of her. The pleasure was so intense that she could only moan and writhe on the bed as Paul pleasured her. His fingers and tongue were so skillful that she knew it wouldn't be long before she climaxed again. She gripped Paul's silky hair, holding on for dear life as the pleasure built. As much as she longed to make it last, the ecstasy was too much, and she could hold back no longer. Her thighs trembled as she peaked, and he lapped at her faster, wanting to draw every ounce of pleasure from her that he could. She collapsed back against the pillows, her breath ragged and her heart racing. He made a soft noise of pleasure and wrapped himself around her, cocooning her as her breathing slowly returned to normal. It wasn't long before she was reaching out for him with a barely sated hunger. Even through his pants, she could feel his desire for her, and she knew that he too needed much more than what they had shared at the beach. She began fumbling with his zipper, making little progress before he became impatient and swatted her hands away. She waited eagerly as he shed all of his clothes, tossing them onto the floor in a heap. He lay on his back next to her, and she grasped his cock eagerly. He looked so sexy, sprawled out before her, naked and eager for her. She took a moment to enjoy his naked form, toned and smooth before taking him into her mouth, delighting in the way he threw his head back and moaned with abandon as she swallowed his member. She closed her eyes as she tongued the underside of the tip, savoring the taste of him. He put his hand under chin, lifting her face slightly.

"Look at me," he said. She opened her eyes again to see him staring down at her with an intensity she had never seen before. His breath quickened, and he stroked her cheek, gazing down at her with open adoration. Keeping her eyes locked on his, she began to work his shaft further and further down her throat, getting a thrill from the look of agonized pleasure on his face. That look emboldened her, made her begin to pick up her pace with enthusiasm, loving the effect she was clearly having on him. As she pleasured Paul with her mouth, but he began to grow dissatisfied with that, shifting his position on the bed so that he was behind her. She could feel his hardness pressing against her folds, but he didn't penetrate her. Instead teased her labia and clit with the tip of his cock. She moaned and squirmed against him, his teasing reigniting the fire inside of her. Her body sought out what it needed, inching him closer and closer to her entrance, desperate to have him inside of her. Hannah felt almost hypnotized, her body tingled with desire, and she longed for Paul to fill her aching pussy. He seemed to be enjoying teasing her, however, rubbing himself against her but never plunging in as she desperately wanted him to.

"What's the matter?" Paul whispered. "Do you want me to fuck you, little one?" She whimpered and nodded. The sensation of his rigid member against her aching sex was driving her wild and she needed satisfaction.

"I'll be happy to oblige you," he teased and then leaned in, growling into her ear. "But you'll have to ask for it." She shivered as he ran the tip of his cock over her clit, rubbing it in slow circles over her swollen nub, breaking down the very last of her inhibitions. Somewhat reluctantly, she took Paul out of her mouth long enough to ask for what she desperately needed.

"Oh Daddy, please fuck me, I need you so bad!" Some part of herself was surprised to hear that kind of language coming out of her mouth, but mostly it only made her feel strangely liberated to give voice to her desires. He plunged into her finally, groaning with satisfaction as he buried himself inside of her to the hilt. Her entire body felt alive as he stretched her open, taking her hard and fast.

"Is that what you wanted, princess?" he moaned into her ear.

"Yes, oh yes," she said enthusiastically. She rocked back to meet his every thrust, lost in a sea of lust and the early blossoming of love. As his thick cock split her open again and again, she could feel another climax building. She reached down to rub her clit, the extra layer of pleasure sending her over the edge. Her whole body quivered as her intense orgasm took her over.

"Good girl," she heard Paul whisper as she moaned wildly around his cock. "You're so tight around my cock. You're going to make me cum, little one!" As Hannah's quaking orgasm began to recede, his thrusts quickened. She could feel his manhood grow even harder inside of her, throbbing on the edge of release. His rhythm suddenly faltered, and his body went rigid. His cock throbbed and twitched inside of her as he filled her up with his seed. Hannah moaned wildly, intoxicated by the sensation. With one final shudder, he collapsed against her and buried his face in her neck.

"Good girl," he whispered shakily, patting the back of her head gently. With a happy grin, she wrapped her arms around him, cradling him. Lying beneath him like that, Hannah felt the happiest she had ever been. His hands glided lovingly over her skin, both soothing and arousing her and Paul kissed her deeply on the lips.

"You are mine now. All mine." She felt her heart melt open in a way it never had before, leaving her feeling raw and vulnerable. Every cell in her body knew it was true, knew that this man was her future.

"All yours," she echoed, her voice hazy with a dreamy contentment. They clung to each other, and she had never felt so safe, so contented. She held him close, kissed his sweaty forehead, and thought about how she would love to stay like that forever.

Chapter 8

Paul had other ideas, however, and his tender caresses grew heated once more. To her surprise, she found that his hunger fueled her own and she found herself already craving more of him. *Who knew I was such a little minx?* It was Paul who brought that out in her, she realized. He buried his face in her breasts, frantically kissing, licking, and sucking her tender flesh. He held her tightly against him as he devoured her, grinding her already wet pussy against him, still slick with their combined juices. Her happy sighs turned to moans as he twisted her body so that he could smack her ass, lightly at first, but then with increasing intensity.

"Do you like it when Daddy spanks you, little one?" he murmured against her nipple. She moaned and squirmed against him, wanting him to continue.

"Yes, Daddy. Spank my ass, please." He grinned up at her and her stomach fluttered with excitement.

"I was hoping you would say that Princess." She gasped in surprise as he pushed her face down onto the bed so that she was on all fours. He rubbed her backside lovingly for a moment, and the anticipation of what would come next made her whine and squirm. Knowing that she was about to get the spanking she had longed for for so long made her go from wet to dripping almost instantly. He slapped her ass forcefully, even harder than he had before. She yelped and jerked at the sharp pain, gritting her teeth as she fought to take it like a good girl. As much as it hurt, it also made her pussy ache. He followed it up with two more swift, sharp blows, making her yelp again. He chuckled at her response and caressed her flesh tenderly with his fingertips.

"What do you think of that, kitten? Do you still like it when Daddy spanks you? Should I keep going?" Her hips automatically thrust back, her buttocks seeking more of the invigorating combination of pleasure and pain. She nodded her head and whimpered, wordlessly asking for more.

"Use your words, kitten," he said sternly, popping her already tender buttcheeks playfully. Even that felt good, even though she craved the harder blows.

"Yes, Daddy," she gasped, overwhelmed by her burning desire. "Please, spank me more!" She hid her face in the pillows of the bed as he delivered blow after blow to her meaty buttocks. She squealed and squirmed as he increased the intensity, each blow landing harder than the last, but she made no move to stop him. Indeed, every blow brought closer to a kind of frenzy, her whole body singing with desire. Suddenly, the onslaught ceased, and he once again stroked her tender flesh, admiring his work. She peeked at him over her shoulder, his face was flushed, and he was breathing heavily, his eyes fixated on her bottom.

"Oh, sweetie, your little bum is so pink," he

said quietly. His fingers on her backside felt so good, and once again, her hips rose, giving him access to all of her. He took the hint and began to lightly trace her cleft, tracing all the way down to the very center of her desire. He gently exploring her folds, holding her gaze with his own as he touched her. The way he stared into her eyes as if he could see her very soul made her heart flutter.

"You're so wet, you dirty little thing. I'm going to have so much fun with you." He twirled his fingertips around her clit, making her eyes roll back in her head. She was so overwhelmed with the sensation that she could neither squeal nor moan, only grip the pillows and writhe on the bed. Just as she thought that it couldn't get more intense, he once again brought his open hand down on her tender rear end. She cried out as she lost all sense of control, surrendering completely to his mastery over her body. He noted her reaction and continued spanking her as he fingered her until she was a gasping, dripping mess.

"You're not about to cum, are you princess?" He smacked her twice in a row, painful smacks that made her jump and gasp, getting ever closer to a powerful orgasm. "Remember, you're mine now. That means you don't cum until I give you permission. Is that understood?"

"Yes, Daddy," she gasped. Her entire body aching at his words. It was so erotic, the thought of him having such absolute control over her body and mind like that, giving or denying pleasure at his whim. He plunged a finger into her aching entrance, bringing her closer to a screaming climax. It took all of her willpower to hold back as he pumped his finger in and out of her, rubbing her most sensitive spot with every stroke. How did he expect her to control herself when he did things like that to her?

"Please, Daddy," she whined. "Please, it feels so good. I want to cum so bad." He didn't seem convinced and spanked her hard, sending sparks of pain and ecstasy all through her. Her tender bottom was beginning to feel raw and bruised, and her body was screaming for release.

"I think you can do better than that, little one."

"Please, Daddy. It feels so good when you spank me and fuck my slutty little pussy. Please, can I cum Daddy, can I?" After all those times she had chastised Claire for using crass language, she couldn't believe that such filth came so easily from her mouth. She found that she didn't care, the dirty words only bringing her closer to the edge. He seemed to love torturing her, sliding a second finger into her, stretching her out. She kicked her legs and squealed, feeling incredibly full and closer than ever to coming without permission. If he didn't give her release soon, she felt she would lose her mind.

"Daddy, please, I can't take it. Please let me cum!"

"Ok, princess, you've been a good girl. You can come for Daddy." He smacked her ass as he pumped his fingers into her, sending Hannah over the edge. Her entire body shook as fingers drove into her relentlessly, demanding more and more with every thrust.

"That's it, kitten. Let it all out. Daddy knows how to take care of this slutty little pussy. There's a good girl." He did not let up until she collapsed against the mattress, panting and utterly spent. He rubbed her butt and back tenderly as she lay there, too exhausted to move. It was as if her entire body had turned to jelly. She couldn't remember ever having cum so hard. She gave a shaky sigh as he removed his fingers and brought them to his mouth, licking them with a satisfied moan. He was so naughty and so sexy. Paul gripped her tender buttocks, delighting in the way it made her whimper and squirm. She could feel his manhood pressing against her dripping pussy, ready to claim her. He didn't seem to be in any particular hurry, however, and took his time kissing her back. She began to moan and writhe against him, her body already on fire again, yearning for more despite the powerful orgasm she'd had just moments before. He wrapped his strong arms around her and held her tightly as he kissed and bit her neck. She thrust her hips up, moaning softly. She felt helpless pinned underneath him like that, and that helplessness was exhilarating.

"Are you already hungry for more, my darling?" he teased playfully as she whined, overwhelmed by her aching need. He moved his hand down to grab the bruised flesh of her buttocks again, digging his fingers into the tender skin as he pulled her closer against his throbbing member. She opened her legs wider as the tip of his cock brushed her labia. He was so close to being inside her, it would take just a tiny little thrust, and she could ease this burning desire within. She felt him run his thumb over her rear entrance and shuddered, totally unprepared for the electric jolt it sent throughout her body.

"What are you doing?" she gasped.

"Do you want me to stop, baby?" he purred.

"No," she shivered, finding that she very much wanted him to keep going. "I like that. It feels really nice." She had never been stimulated there before, had never even given it much thought, but as Paul ran circles around her rear entrance, it made her pussy react strongly. He dipped his thumb into her slick juices giving his thumb more slip as he slowly began to sink it in, moving gradually to allow her body time to adjust to the new intrusion. After a moment, he began to work it in and out of her, and she squealed and squirmed with delight.

"Oh, Daddy," she cried out, too lost in lust to be bashful any longer. "Daddy, please fuck my ass." Just as she was beginning to think that she might climax again just from his thumb in her rear, Paul pulled it out of her ass and replaced it with the tip of his member. Slowly, he began to push himself into her, stretching out her rear end with his thick cock. As he began to fill her, Hannah screamed and thrashed underneath him. It felt more amazing than anything she had ever experienced before. As he inched his way in, she was fascinated by delicious combination of pain and pleasure, and she only wanted more and more. He was slick with her juices and slid in easily yet was careful not to go too quickly lest he hurt her. He pushed himself past the rim, her tight ass hugging the tip of his cock. She thrust her hips back, wanting to take more of him inside of her. He let her control the pace, letting her fuck herself deeper and deeper with his cock. She thrust herself all the way back, taking him completely inside her body. Paul took that as a green light and began to pound into her. She surrendered herself to him and held on as he unleashed his passion for her, thrusting into her hard and fast. He gripped her hips, pulling her back so that he could bury himself in her back passage. Hannah could feel her orgasm building, knew it would be long before it came crashing over her and she would be powerless to stop it. Before she could even form a thought, she was already coming again. Her eyes rolled back, and she cried out, louder than ever before, coming totally undone as he brought her to greater heights of pleasure than she ever knew was possible.

"Oh, fuck. You're so tight. Am I the first one

to fuck your ass?"

"Yes, Daddy," she moaned. "Fuck my virgin ass, please!" It seemed that she couldn't take any more pleasure as he thrust into her over and over. They both moaned and writhed together, lost in a bliss that felt so good and so right that she also didn't ever want it to be over. Paul went over the edge once more, biting down on her shoulder as he stiffened and filled her with his seed again. She shivered with delight at the feeling of being so full of his warm semen and moaned with satisfaction as he collapsed into a sweaty, breathless heap on top of her. Neither of them could speak; they could only hold each other closely. Sated at last, they basked in their contentment. She was sure that she was the luckiest woman alive and that she had the most wonderful man on the planet right here with her.

Chapter 9

"Would you like me to put you in a diaper?" he asked. Hannah had been very close to falling asleep, but the suggestion made her sit straight up. The thought of having yet another fantasy fulfilled this evening made her heart pound. He really was her dream come to life.

"Yes, Daddy, I would like that very much." His face lit up, and he went into his closet, rummaging around until he came back with a pack of diapers.

"I've been saving these," he said. "Hoping to have the opportunity to use them one day."

"You've never diapered anyone before?" she asked.

"No," he shook his head. "This will be my first time." She grinned at that, suddenly feeling very proud to be his first. It also put her more at ease, knowing that she wasn't the only one experiencing all of this for the first time. He took the diaper out of the package and gently spread her knees open with his hands.

"Hips up, little one," he said and slid the diaper underneath her. He took a moment to admire her naked form before fastening the diaper closed. "You're so beautiful, princess. Do you ever wet your diaper?"

"I do," she admitted shyly. "Especially at night."

"Good girl," he grinned, patting the front of her diaper approvingly. "In that case, I expect to see a very full diaper in the morning, is that understood?"

"Yes, Daddy," she said, returning her grin. It felt like such a relief to not only be open about her lifestyle around him but to share it with him as well. It was so liberating to know that he not only tolerated it, he craved it as much as she did. He rejoined her on the bed and wrapped her in his arms once again. She burrowed her face into his chest, savoring his masculine scent.

"Sorry that I don't have any stuffies or anything else that a little might enjoy. I'll go pick up some things tomorrow while you're out."

"That's ok, Daddy. You can be my stuffie tonight," she said, stifling a yawn. He chuckled and kissed her forehead.

"Sounds like it's bedtime for you, little one. Get a good night's sleep."

"You too, Daddy." He held her tightly as she drifted off to sleep with a happy smile on her face.

***

When she awoke, Paul was still asleep. The pressure on her bladder told her that she had not yet wet herself as she had promised. She released her urine into the diaper, soaking it thoroughly. As the warm liquid soaked into the absorbent fabric, she thought her new Daddy would be very pleased with her, and it filled her with pride. She took a moment to admire his handsome face as he slept.

It felt so nice to finally have a Daddy that she could call her very own. She had dreamed of this for so long, and it was finally here. Some part of her still felt like this was all just a wonderful dream. At last, Paul began to stir. She placed a gentle kiss on his cheek, and his eyes fluttered open.

"Good morning, princess," he whispered. "Did you sleep well?"

"Yes, Daddy. I need you to change me, please." He opened his eyes wider and smiled at her. He had such a lovely smile, she thought. Even lovelier when it was because of her.

"Oh, is that so? Let me see." He lifted the covers and peeked at her puffy, full diaper. With one hand, he reached down and patted the front approvingly. "Yes, you did a very good job, little one. Daddy is very proud of you." He peeled the covers off of her and fished around for some baby wipes. As he unfastened the tabs and pulled her diaper down, he took in a deep breath.

"Yes, that's what I was hoping to see. You did a very good job, princess."

"Thank you, Daddy," she said, blushing and glowing with pride at the same time. She lifted her hips so that he could slide the soiled diaper from beneath her. He bundled it up and tossed it in the trash. Taking a wipe from the pack, he lovingly cleaned her. The soft material felt so good against her pussy, and it felt even better to be so tenderly pampered.

"Would you like to take a shower with me, pumpkin?" he asked as he tossed the wipe away.

"Mmm, that sounds nice," she smiled. He took her by the hands and helped her onto her feet. He took a moment to wrap her tightly in his arms, their naked, warm bodies pressed against one another. Then, he took her by the hand and led her into the bathroom. After getting the water temperature just right, he pulled her under the stream with him. He washed her from head to toe, lovingly sudsing up every inch of her body and then rinsing her clean again. As he bathed her, his cock came to life, and Hannah wanted so badly to taste him. Paul caught her peeking and stroked his cock seductively as she watched.

"I know you want to suck my cock," he teased. "Isn't that right, my dirty little princess?" She watched, hypnotized, as he slowly stroked his member, never once taking his eyes off of her naked body. She could only nod, feeling dazed and speechless with lust. He laughed, clearly enjoying the mesmerizing effect he was having over her.

"Get on your knees," he growled, and she obeyed instantly, warm water cascading over her body as she knelt before him. She took his juicy member in her hands, a shiver of excitement going through her. She guided his throbbing cock to her lips, moaning with pleasure as she tasted him.

"I told you last night to look at me when you suck my cock," he barked, and she looked up to meet his gaze. "Good little slut. Keep your eyes on me. Remember who you belong to." His words set her on fire, and she began to bob her head up and down on his erection. She took more and more of him down her throat, her excitement, and eagerness to please him, lowering her inhibitions.

No matter how far down her throat she was able to take him, she still craved more, choking herself with his throbbing cock over and over.

"Slow down," he whispered. "I'm not done with you yet." He pulled her to her feet and pushed her face-first against the bathroom tile. He pulled her hands behind her, holding both of her wrists with one hand as he slapped her ass hard, sending a jolt of pain and pleasure through her that left her weak in the knees and blind with lust. Her ass was slightly bruised from the night before, and he took his time, adding a few more bruises until she was whimpering and squirming. He ran his hand lightly over her tender buttocks, growling with satisfaction.

"Oh baby, you look so perfect," he whispered. "Now you're marked by me, and you'll always have a reminder that you're my baby girl." She shivered. That feeling of belonging to him was so intoxicating, and her body cried out for him, wanting him to claim her yet again. He slid his finger inside her needy pussy first, and it felt so good that she saw stars. She moaned loudly, bucking her hips back.

"You like that, huh? Naughty little slut." He pulled his finger out, replacing it with the tip of his cock, and slowly began to push in. She hissed with satisfaction as he slowly eased himself in, stretching her open inch by inch. With a fierce growl, he rammed himself the rest of the way into her. She gasped and collapsed against the tile wall, letting herself get totally lost in the pleasure. He slammed into her harder and harder, and she could feel herself building to a climax.

"Oh fuck, Daddy. You're going to make me cum!" she cried out.

"You'd better not, little one. I want you to be desperate and horny for me all day long. I want this little cunt of yours to be so drippy and needy that you can't wait to get off work and rush over to be my little fuck-slave again." Again she wondered how he expected her not to cum all over his cock when he said deliciously nasty things like that to her. Suddenly, he gripped her hips harder, pulling her back against him. With his throbbing cock buried deep inside of her, he let out a roar and pumped her full of his hot cum. It was so hard not to cum with him, but she held herself back, eager to be a good girl for him. As he pulled out of her, she could only twitch and moan quietly. Even after being denied an orgasm, she felt more satisfied than she ever had before. Just knowing that she had pleased him made her happy, and she looked forward to a day of burning for more of him. She could feel his hot semen dripping out and shivered with delight at the sensation. It felt so good to be full of him, to know that she served him well. He put his hand under her chin, pulling her face to his for a gentle kiss. She bathed him in the same way that he had bathed her. Running her hands over sudsy muscles only made the ache between her legs more intense, but she found that she enjoyed the ache. As he had said earlier, it reminded her who she belonged to and that was the best feeling in the world.

Chapter 10

He dropped her off at work a few hours later. At first, she assumed she would take his spare car, but he said that he wanted to spend the extra time with her. As he drove her, he casually fondled her, stroking her pussy and tweaking her nipples so that she was burning with desire for him with no possible source of relief. She whined that it wasn't fair, but secretly she hoped that he wouldn't stop. It was as cruel as it was hot. After he dropped her off with a deep passionate kiss, she filled in Claire on all the developments that had happened since she last saw her. As she recapped the surfing competition, their night on the couch together, and their trip to the private beach, Claire hung onto her every word.

"Wait, wait. So you're telling me that you two are together now?!" Hannah blushed, thinking to herself that Claire didn't even know the half of it. Together didn't even begin to describe what was happening between her and Paul.

"Yeah, I guess we are," she giggled, knowing that Claire would never really understand even if she did explain it.

"Ugh, you lucky bitch. Did you two do it yet?" Hannah wasn't used to sharing such intimate details, even with friends, but the deep blush that came over her face told Claire everything she needed to know. She jumped up and down, squealing and clapping. "Oh my god, it's about time you got some. How was it?"

"Um, it was - "Hannah was saved by the bell, or rather by her cell phone ringing. She held up a finger to Claire as she answered it.

"Tell me later," Claire mouthed and went outside to meet her group.

"Hello?"

"Hello, this Bob Chance with the Brighter Day Aquarium. "I got your information from Mr. Peterson. He was quite enthusiastic about your capabilities, and he is a difficult man to impress. We were hoping that you would be willing to come in for an interview." Hannah struggled not to whoop for joy and somehow managed to schedule a time to meet with Mr. Chance without squealing or babbling too much. As she hung up the phone, tears of joy and gratitude streamed down her face. He had never even mentioned that he'd put in a good word for her, and here she was with an interview for her dream job all lined up. If she thought she was going to be counting down the minutes until she got off work before, it was going to be sheer torture now. She couldn't wait to get back to Paul's to show him just how grateful she truly was.

"Come on, Hannah, your group is waiting," Mr. Williams poked his head into the breakroom, looking sweaty and annoyed. Hannah looked up at him in surprise and wiped a tear from her eye, and he quickly softened. "Oh hey, don't cry about it." Hannah shook her head and chuckled slightly, realizing that she probably looked a mess.

"It's not you, Mr. Williams. I just got some good news."

"Oh, well congratulations then, I guess. Tell you what, take a minute to pull yourself together. I'll tell them you're in the bathroom with a stomach ache or something." He was gone before she could point out that they might not want to be in the water with someone with a stomach ache. She shook her head with a smile as she went into the bathroom to splash water on her face before going out to give what would hopefully be one of her last dolphin tours.

***

Paul was already waiting for her in the parking lot, and she ran out to greet him with a huge smile on her face.

"Guess what," she gushed, too excited to even giving him a chance to guess. "I got a call from Mr. Chance today, and I have an interview with him in two days."

"That's fantastic news!" he exclaimed and wrapped her in a huge bear hug. "Looks like we have something to celebrate tonight. Other than finding each other that is." The last part, he whispered in her ear, and it sent a shiver of delight through her. She had been on a cloud of happiness and horniness all day, and now, with his body pressed against her, the heat that had been building all day suddenly overwhelmed her. He kissed her forehead and opened the car door for her. As he got into the driver's seat, he started the car but didn't put it into gear. He turned to her, a look of predatory hunger on his face.

"Have you been thinking about being my little fuck-slave all day like I told you to?" he asked, reaching over to put his hand over her crotch. She shuddered and groaned at his touch.

"Yes, Daddy," she whispered, her eyes fluttering closed.

"Show me," he demanded. "Pull down your shorts." She took a nervous look around before unbuttoning her shorts and sliding them down over her hips and onto the floorboard. He pushed aside her bathing suit bottom and dipped his finger between her moist folds. "Oh baby girl, you are so wet."

"I've been tingling for you all day," she sighed. He sat back with a smile and pulled his finger back. He snickered at the way she whimpered.

"Show Daddy again where the tingles are," he said with a wicked glint in his eyes. Again, she looked out of the window nervously.

"But what if someone sees?" she asked.

"Then they'll see a good little slut who does what she's told," he growled, totally unconcerned. "Show me right now." His eyes followed her every movement as she pulled her bathing suit farther to the side and parted her folds for him to see.

"Touch your clit." She put her finger on her sensitive spot as he watched her closely.

"Good girl. Now stroke it." She did as he said, twirling her finger around her swollen clit and moaning softly as it sent ripples of pleasure all through her body. Already, she felt ready to explode at a moment's notice.

"Like that, Daddy?" she asked, as eager to please him as she was to release her pent up desire.

"Slower, baby girl. I don't want you to cum just yet. You're so cute when you squirm and whine." She slowed her pace as he instructed, the slower pace amplifying every sensation, making her entire body ache for more.

"Yes, Daddy," she sighed, delighting yet again at the control he had over her body and her pleasure. "I'll be a good girl."

"I know you will. You're Daddy's good girl." He watched with silent fascination as she fingered herself and moaned softly.

"Stop," he said suddenly. She took my finger away but stuck out her bottom lip, which only made him grin wickedly. "So cute. You want to cum so badly don't you, my greedy little princess?"

"Yes, Daddy," she whined.

"Good girl, that's how Daddy likes you.

Now, put your finger inside that tight little pussy of yours." She sank her finger into her eager hole, seeking out the sweet spot under his watchful eye. As she found it, she sighed with pleasure and let her eyes roll back in her head.

"Does that feel good, pumpkin?" His voice was so thick with lust that it too added another layer to her pleasure.

"Yes, Daddy. That feels so good, thank you for letting me finger my greedy pussy."

"You're welcome, baby girl. Now, move it in and out slowly. And remember, no cumming yet." She moved her finger in and out of her aching pussy as slowly as she could. He looked absolutely ready to devour her, but he only watched her patiently, seemingly in no rush at all. "I know that greedy pussy is aching for more. Use two fingers." She swallowed and put a second finger inside, inching it in slowly. She could feel herself stretch open to accommodate it, and it felt so delicious that she let her head roll back and moaned loudly, no longer concerned about who might see or hear.

"See kitten? I know what that slutty little pussy of yours needs. Isn't that right?"

"Yes, Daddy knows," she said, knowing that it was true.

"Daddy knows about what?" he teased. She shivered, loving the way he made her say the dirtiest things.

"Daddy knows what my slutty little pussy needs," she gasped, her voice taking on a high pitched, pleading quality.

"Daddy?"

"Yes, baby girl?" He never took his eyes off her fingers as they went in and out of her dripping pussy.

"Can I cum? I need to cum. Pretty please?" She hoped that if she asked very nicely, he would grant her request, and she would finally be able to find relief from this burning need.

"You're a good girl for asking first. But no." She groaned in disappointment as he put the car into reverse.

"Daddy, please!" she cried but he only

shook his head.

"Not until we get home, little one. That doesn't mean you can stop playing with yourself, though. Put on your seatbelt, and then I want you to edge all the way home. And then, you're going to get it, little one."

Chapter 11

Hannah somehow managed to hold on until they pulled into Paul's driveway.

"Get inside, little one. Daddy has been waiting for this all day." She practically skipped to his front door, eager to end her torture at last. As he opened the door, she noticed that he had an armful of shopping bags.

"What's that?" she asked curiously, suddenly remembering his promise of presents.

"Nevermind, I'll show you later," he said, putting them down by the door. "Now get on your knees and show Daddy how much you missed me."

"I missed so much, Daddy," she said, kneeling before him obediently.

"I missed you too, pumpkin." He smiled down at her and pulled his cock out, stroking it slowly as she watched with greedy fascination.

"Now open that pretty little mouth." Eagerly, she opened wide, moaning happily at the taste of him as he slid his erection on to her soft, wet tongue.

"I've been thinking about this hot little mouth all day," he groaned and grabbed the back of her head firmly. Holding her in place, he eased his cock further down her throat until she began to gag. She remembered to look up at him as he penetrated her throat. Her pussy was dripping wet as she enjoyed the look of ecstasy on his handsome face, knowing how much pleasure she was bringing him. He stroked her face tenderly as he forced his cock deeper down her throat, smiling at the way she choked on him, whispering encouragement as he pushed her to her limits.

"That's it, baby. Keep that mouth open, let Daddy fuck that pretty little face" he said as he pulled out. Drool dribbled down her chin and chest, staining her swimsuit. He smiled down at her, enjoying the sight of her getting dirty to please him.

"Did you like choking on my cock, baby

girl?" She nodded, obediently keeping her mouth open. He placed the head of his cock on her tongue again but didn't push in. "Do you want some more?"

"Uh-huh," she nodded again.

"Good girl," he growled, and he thrust himself deep into her throat. She moaned and gurgled as he slid down her throat, his thick erection cutting off her air supply. As she held her breath, she noticed how it intensified every sensation and made her pussy ache for relief. He began to pull back, but she grabbed his hips, not wanting to let go just yet. He watched with loving fascination as she struggled to keep him down. He pulled out just as she was beginning to get light-headed and stroked his cock, watching her gasp for air.

"You're such a good little cocksucker, aren't you baby girl?" he asked, wiping a bit of drool from her chin. She nodded and swallowed.

"Yes, Daddy. I love sucking your cock." She was glowing with pride at his praise, proud to be a good slut for him.

"Good girl," he purred. "You're so sexy, little one. I love watching you choke on me. Ready for some more?"

"Yes, please," she grinned and opened her mouth wide. He sank his cock in, even deeper than before. She relaxed into it, so lost in her haze of lust and obedience that she swallowed him completely. He set a hypnotizing pace, fucking her throat slowly but steadily. The rougher he got, the more her pussy tingled and dripped with desire. She kept my hands at her sides even though she ached to cum with his cock down her throat. She swallowed his cock over and over, hoping that she would earn the privilege of cumming soon.

"Oh, princess, you're going to make me cum. Are you going to be a good girl and swallow it?"

"Yes, Daddy," she squealed with delight. "I want to swallow all of your yummy cum!" With a grunt, he thrust himself down her throat, and she opened wide as she felt his cock pulse. He shouted as he came and pushed himself deeper still into her throat. She struggled not to choke and managed to swallow every bit of it down just as she had promised.

"Oh, baby," he said, gently pulling himself out of her mouth. "You're such a good girl, I'm so proud of you."

"Thank you, Daddy," she said.

"I think you've earned yourself an orgasm, little one. Why don't you take off that swimsuit and come sit on Daddy's face." She quickly shed her suit, eager to have the chance to finally cum at last. He led her over to the couch, lying on his back and pulling her on top of him so that she was straddling his face. He gave her pussy a long slow lick, moaning with delight as he tasted her. She moaned with relief as he finally gave her aching pussy the attention it had been begging and ground her hips against him. He grabbed her by the wrists and moved her hands to her bare breasts.

"Play with those perfect titties, kitten," he

whispered. "Give Daddy a little show." He went back to twirling his tongue around her clit as she obeyed, pinching her nipples as he watched her closely.

"Harder," he commanded. "I know you can take it." She twisted her nipple as hard as she could, the pain combining with the delicious sensations of his tongue lapping at her and she moaned, grinding herself against his mouth. His fingers dug into the flesh of her ass as he devoured her, bringing another layer of delightful sensation.

"Slap your tits," he growled and flicked his tongue lightly across her clit. Tentatively, she smacked her palms on her nipples, intrigued by the sensation. "Harder. I want to watch your tits get as red as your ass." She slapped her breasts with more and more force, each time the pain mixed with pleasure brought her closer to a climax. He groaned approvingly and smack her ass hard, almost making her lose control.

"Please, Daddy," she cried out. "Please I need to cum so bad!"

"I know, baby girl. You can cum for Daddy now." She moaned with sweet relief as she squirmed against his mouth. He brought his hand down onto her fleshy buttock once more, and she could hold back no longer. Instinctively, she twisted her nipples, harder than ever before as she came, wave after wave of intense pleasure washing over her. He held her firmly down on his tongue as she shivered and quaked, her moans echoing off through the entire house. As she collapsed back, he caught her, gently easing her down on the couch. She sighed happily as he kissed her deeply. She could taste her own juices on his tongue, and she moaned into his mouth, feeling delightfully naughty. She loved the way she never felt inhibited around him, the way he was opening her up to a whole new world of pleasure. To her surprise, Paul was already hard again. Eating her out must have aroused him once more because she could feel him begin to press into her, ready to claim her again. With a sigh, he grabbed her by the hips and flipped her so that she was up on all fours. She was still sensitive from her climax and shivered with ecstasy as he thrust into her. She moaned and pushed back to meet him, taking him deeper inside of her, still craving more of him. She didn't think she would ever get enough of him.

"Daddy, you feel so good," she cried out, thrashing her head against the pillow as he split her open again and again. He grabbed her hand, guiding it to touch her clit as he pounded into her.

"Do you want to cum again, princess?" he asked.

"Yes, Daddy," she said, rubbing her clit frantically as his hard cock stretched her out.

"Oh princess, you're milking my cock so good. You're so tight and wet, just for me, isn't that right?"

"Just for you, Daddy," she agreed.

"That's right, Daddy's little greedy slut who just wants to cum on his cock, again and again, right kitten?"

"Yes, Daddy. I want to cum on your cock. Can I, please?"

"Yes, baby girl. You've been such a good slut for Daddy today. You can cum again if you want to." She couldn't answer, she could only moan and rub her clit as she clenched around his cock, climaxing with such force that her legs shook.

"Good girl," he growled and hammered into her even harder. As the waves of ecstasy, receded she pulled her hand away from her clit, but that earned her a hard slap on the ass, making her yelp with pain. He roughly grabbed her by the wrist and replaced her hand between her legs.

"I didn't tell you to stop touching yourself, now did I baby girl?" he growled, smacking her ass again. Hannah's eyes rolled back in her head, the thoughts in her head thoroughly scrambled.

"N-no, Daddy," she managed to stammer out. Obediently, she ran her finger over her swollen clit once again, overwhelmed with pleasure as he claimed her body with his.

"You did such a good job holding back, but now I don't want you to stop cumming until you can't think or stand." She shivered as the image made her toes curl. Already, she felt unable to form words or thoughts. As she grunted and thrust back against him, she felt more like her true self than she ever had before. It felt so right and natural to give over control to him, to be his slave made only to please him. The thought made her pussy clench, and she knew that she would soon be orgasming again, just as he had commanded.

"Oh Daddy," she squealed and came so hard that her voice broke, and her legs collapsed beneath her. Paul just kept right on fucking her into the couch without mercy. She kicked her legs and squealed, the stimulation was too much to handle, and she felt like she was losing her mind.

"Such a good slut," He groaned and swatted her ass again. "Keep rubbing that clit, little one. I'm not going to tell you again." Hannah obeyed at once, not wanting to find out what was behind that veiled threat. She rubbed her clit, helpless against the onslaught of pleasure as Paul continued to use her roughly, just the way she liked it. She whined and moaned, her skin growing slick with sweat as she thrashed and kicked underneath him. No one had ever fucked her so thoroughly before, had certainly never engaged her mind or emotions as they fucked her the way that he did. As overstimulated as she felt, she also didn't want it to end. Just as she was beginning to think that she couldn't handle cumming one more time, she could feel Paul stiffening inside of her, and she knew that he was about to go over the edge again.

"Oh baby girl, you're doing so good, keep taking it just like that," he cried out, grabbing a fist full of her hair for purchase as he slammed into her. The pain in her scalp combined with the hot cum he was pumping into her pussy made her shake with an orgasm so powerful that she couldn't even make noise. She could only shiver and quake beneath him. It seemed to last forever, but at last, she collapsed against the couch, utterly spent. He, too, collapsed onto the couch, curling himself around her as they regained their breath. *He got his wish;* she thought to herself as the idea of moving or even thinking seemed impossible.

She felt like her entire body had turned to jelly. She was sore and exhausted but also happier than she had ever felt in her life. Paul wrapped his arm around her waist, pulling her close.

"Oh princess, you are so perfect. Daddy is so proud of you." He held her face up to his for a kiss, his warm lips gentle and soft against hers. She melted into him, savoring the warm feeling of skin on skin.

Chapter 12

Eventually, he disentangled himself from her with a groan, stretching languidly before getting up to grab the shopping bags that were still waiting by the door.

"Are you ready for your presents, little one?" He set the bags in front of her, and she could feel the energy returning to her limbs as if by magic. She sat up on the couch and clapped her hands excitedly.

"Yes!" she cried. "Gimme, gimme." He laughed and picked up one of the bags and set it on her lap.

"Go ahead," he prompted, and she tore into the bag to find a treasure trove of stuffed animals, coloring books and crayons, and pacifiers for her to enjoy. "I wanted to pick up a few things that you can leave here. I want to make sure that you feel completely at home when you sleepover." She felt her heart melt as she looked from the pile of toys to his warm, sincere eyes. She reached out and touched his face, suddenly wanting to make sure that he was real and that all of this hadn't been just a beautiful dream.

"I love it. I do feel at home here with you." He smiled and grabbed her hand, pulling it to his lips for a tender kiss.

"Glad to hear it," he said, his voice thick with emotion. He stood and scooped her up from the couch, making her squeal and giggle as he swung her up into his arms. "Come on, let's get you diapered up, and you can play while I make us dinner." He carried her to the bedroom and placed her gently on the bed. He took a moment to admire her as she opened her legs for him.

"Fuck, baby girl, you look so sexy with my cum leaking out of you. You couldn't be any more perfect." He took a wet wipe and began to delicately clean her off, moving it slowly over her pussy as his breath began to quicken. It filled her with such pride, knowing that he was already hungry for her again, even after she had pleasured him so many times. He slid a fresh diaper under her and fastened it with elastic tabs.

"I have an old t-shirt you can wear," he said, going into his closet to select one for her. "I suppose we'll have to bring some extra clothes over here as well." She giggled. "That reminds me, we'd better wash that bathing suit before I go back to work tomorrow after we got it so dirty." He smirked and tossed her a clean t-shirt. "I suppose you're right. Totally worth it, though."

"Totally worth it," she agreed, sliding his t-shirt over her head and standing up. His eyes lit up as he looked at her.

"You can keep all the fancy lingerie in the world," he said, looking her up and down admiringly. "You've never looked more beautiful and sexy than you do right now. I wish you could always just be in a diaper and my shirt." He grabbed her by the ass, patting her diapered behind lovingly, making her giggle and blush. He picked her up once again and carried her into the living room and put her down on the floor. She loved the way he carried her around all the time. It made her feel so little and protected. He fished around in the bag for a pacifier and placed it gently in her mouth, then laid her coloring supplies and a couple of stuffies on the floor next to her. He watched her play for a few minutes, helping her decide the names of new stuffed animal friends, before wandering off to the kitchen to make their dinner.

***

"I have another surprise for you," he said over dinner, making her eyes go wide in surprise.

"Another one?!" He laughed and took her hand, squeezing it affectionately.

"I got the call today that your car is finally ready. I was beginning to worry that it wouldn't be ready until after your graduation ceremony, but we can pick it up tomorrow. When is your graduation, by the way?"

"In three days, the day after my interview come to think of it." Her brow wrinkled with worry as she began to remember all of her real-life responsibilities. Interviews had always made her nervous, even when they were just the kind of low paying jobs that had put her through school. Now that she was faced with interviewing for her dream job, her stomach curdled with anxiety. Paul saw her expression change and reached out for her hand again. His touch did soothe her, she noticed.

"Hey," he said softly. "You have nothing to worry about. They're going to love you just as much as I do." Her face turned red, but she did feel calmer after his reassuring words. She smiled and tried to put the worry out of her mind.

"Thank you, Daddy," she said softly.

"What would you like to do to celebrate your new job? Big party?" He winked, knowing full well how little she liked parties. She laughed and shook her head.

"Absolutely nothing," she said. "I've been working for so hard and for so long that all I want now is a day where I do absolutely nothing."

"Done," he said. "Call in sick to work tomorrow. I'll wait on you hand and foot. You won't have to lift a finger for the whole day." She looked at him, completely surprised that he had taken her joke so seriously.

"Really?" The thought was tempting, sure, but she couldn't expect him to do everything for her for an entire day, could she?

"Really and truly," he said. "Let me take care of you. I want to, and you deserve it."

"Ok," she said with a grin. "I'll let Mr. Williams know right away." She took out her phone to type out a text, but he took it from her hands.

"Actually, let's not wait for tomorrow. Starting now, I'll take care of everything you need, including texting your boss. All you have to worry about is coming up with things for me to get you or do for you. Or to you." He winked again and turned his attention to typing out the message. Once again, she found herself wondering what she could have done to deserve such a wonderful man. It seemed impossible to her that he could be so aggressive in the bedroom and so kind to her the rest of the time. She didn't think she could have created a more perfect man if she had tried.

"All set," he said with a grin, handing her phone back to her. "What is your first command, my princess?"

"Read me a story!" she said, naming the first thing that popped into her head.

"I seem to recall a certain book that you were going to borrow. Want me to read you that one?" She nodded, getting even more excited at the idea. She had gotten so wrapped up in the events of the past few days that she had completely forgotten about that book.

"Ok, princess, let's go upstairs." He picked her up from the table and carried her to the bedroom. He placed her gently on the bed and then went to fetch the book. After tucking her in, he snuggled up next to her on the bed and found the page that she had marked when she had last read it.

"No, go back some, I don't remember what happened," she said.

"Yes, ma'am," he said and went back to the beginning of the chapter. She lay back and closed her eyes, listening to his deep, velvety voice. She stifled a yawn, not wanting to admit even to herself that she was sleepy. She wanted to listen to him read forever. Try as she might; however, she couldn't fight off sleep as the exhaustion from a long day at work on top of their marathon lovemaking finally caught up with her. Paul waited until her breaths were long and even to make sure that she was asleep before he slipped out of bed as quietly as he could to go clean up the kitchen.

Chapter 13

She awoke sometime later to something brushing between her legs. She opened her eyes to see Paul putting his hand down her diaper. She moaned and opened her legs, ready for him in an instant. He kissed her as he fingered her pussy, further igniting her desire.

"You're already wet," he noted with satisfaction. "You just need more of Daddy's cock."

"I sure do, Daddy. That is definitely next on my princess list." She ran her fingers through his silky black hair as he twirled his tongue around hers. Impatiently, he ripped her diaper off her and tossed it aside. As he settled between her legs, she noted that he was already naked and ready for her. He began to trail sloppy kisses down her neck and breasts, working his way down her body until his face was buried between her legs. With a happy sigh, he gave her pussy a long, slow lick, twirling his tongue sensually around her swollen clit. She threw her head back against the pillow and moaned as he expertly pleasured her.

"That's it, pumpkin," he said, sliding a finger into her. "Let Daddy take care of this needy little pussy." He resumed his attention to her clit. He reached his free hand up to grab her breast and pinched her nipple as she had done earlier. They were still sore from the abuse she had inflicted on them, and it stung all the more as he squeezed them harder and harder. The combined sensations of pleasure and pain drew her closer to orgasm, and she squirmed against his mouth, not sure how much leeway her princess day would allow her. She whined and kicked her legs, holding herself back just in case. Just then, he stopped and repositioned himself so that he was on top of her, his hardness pressing against her aching pussy. He kissed her deeply as his hands circled her wrists, holding them down onto the mattress gently but firmly. She loved it when he held her down like that, keeping her in place as his cock slowly worked its way into position. She loved being reminded of his control over her.

"Do you like cumming on Daddy's cock, little one?" he asked sweetly, pressing himself against her entrance.

"I love cumming on your cock, Daddy. It feels so good when you fuck me."

"I'm glad to hear it. Since it's your princess day, you can cum whenever you like, ok pumpkin?"

"Oh, thank you, Daddy," she moaned as he inched his cock inside of her. "You're so good to me." She nearly sang with delight as he began to sink his cock further inside of her, still holding her firmly down by the wrists. He entered her so painfully slow that she tried to thrust her hips upwards to take more of him in, but he had his weight positioned so that she couldn't move. No matter which way she squirmed, she was pinned in place beneath him. He continued that excruciatingly slow pace until he was buried inside of her completely, holding himself there for a moment before pulling out again at that same incredibly slow speed.

"Daddy," she whined, futilely kicking her legs. "What are you doing?"

"What do you mean," he said, his voice heavy with fake innocence. "You asked for Daddy's cock, so I'm letting you have it." She groaned as he sank back into her, filling her up inch by excruciating inch.

"Please," she cried out "I need you to fuck me!"

"But sweetheart, I am fucking you." His voice still had that fake, syrupy-sweet innocence as though he had no idea that she was on the verge of tears, desperate for the hard pounding she beginning to grow accustomed to.

"Please, Daddy," she said, thrashing my head back and forth on the pillow. His slow torture was too much, and she felt like she might explode. "I need you to fuck me hard. I need you to pound me with your cock. Pound my pussy, Daddy. Give it to me!"

"Your wish is my command, princess," he said with a happy growl and unleashed himself onto her. Still holding her down by the wrists, he finally gave her the fucking that she had begged for. He pounded into her so hard and fast that every thrust made her go mad with pleasure. She did not last long, coming undone beneath him. She grabbed his hips and held on as her body seized with ecstasy. He growled and pumped into her even more furiously as she clenched around him. Even as she relaxed against the sheets, her orgasm waning, he did not lessen his pace. His breath grew faster, panting and growling in her ear as the onslaught of pleasure continued. She could still feel waves of pleasure with every wild thrust, almost like aftershocks. She knew that if he kept fucking her this way, she would be cumming again very soon. She loved seeing him unleashed like this, loved knowing that she made him lose control. He released her hands so that he could grab her breasts, squeezing them so tightly that she gasped.

"I love how tight you get when I do that. Daddy's greedy little pain slut." His words made her tighten around him even more, and she could feel his muscles begin to tense, knew that he was getting closer to his climax as well. As he drove himself deep inside of her with one final thrust, she exploded around him. He flooded her pussy with his hot cum waves of pure joy and ecstasy overtook her. They shouted as they came together and fell back in a panting, sweaty heap.

"Oh baby girl," he whispered and pulled her close. "You're so much more than I ever could have dreamed of. I'm so glad I found you." He held her and kissed her for a while until she began to yawn again. It had grown dark as she slept, and she wondered vaguely what time it was.

"Get some more sleep, princess. I'll be right here when you wake up."

Chapter 14

The rest of her princess day went by in a happy daze, as though she were living in a beautiful dream. Paul served her a huge breakfast in bed, even going to far as to feed her one bite at a time. There were eggs, toast, coffee, and fruit, so much that she couldn't even finish it all.

"I told you you weren't going to lift a finger today, and I meant it," he had said as he fed her fork full after fork full. After breakfast, they lay in bed for a while, just cuddling and chatting. Eventually, he diapered her and carried her downstairs so that they could watch cartoons on the couch. As they relaxed, she got an email informing her that she had aced her last final and would be graduating with honors after all. Paul insisted on cracking open a bottle of champagne in celebration of the wonderful news despite the early hour. She giggled as the bubbles tickled her nose, and it really did seem as though she were living in a dream, a happy dream that she hoped she never woke up from. The bubbly alcohol only added to her giddiness, and she giggled at nothing like a mad woman. They made a picnic on the floor for lunch. Paul put together a simple meal of sandwiches and orange slices. After they ate, they made love again, their fingers and lips still sticky from the citrus fruit. Her body ached from so much lovemaking but still, she wanted more of him. Afterward, she colored on the floor while he read on the couch, both of them enjoying the quiet time together. Later that afternoon, he drove her to her house so that she could prepare for her interview. He quizzed her with mock interview questions as she modeled various outfits for him. Eventually, she settled on one and laid it out for the morning. Once she felt thoroughly prepared for the interview, he insisted that she get into bed early so that she would be nice and rested the next morning.

"I thought it was my princess day and that I could do anything I wanted," she objected. He kissed her nose.

"It may be your princess day, but Daddy is still in charge, understood?"

"Yes, Daddy," she conceded. "But I'm not sleepy yet."

"Do you want me to bring you some dinner?" he offered, but she shook her head.

"No, I think I'm too nervous to eat."

"Hmm," he thought for a moment before pulling out his phone. "I think I have just the thing." A few taps later, he pulled up a soothing music playlist, complete with babbling brooks and chirping birds. He set that off the side and then scooped her up into his lap, rocking her gently as he held her. She closed her eyes, relaxing into his warm embrace.

"It's all going to be ok, little one. You are going to get this job. I just know it. You're the smartest, sweetest girl I've ever met, and they'd be absolutely insane not to hire you. So just rest your little head and quit worrying." The rocking motion was incredibly soothing, and his embrace was so warm. She felt so safe in his arms that the nervousness began to melt away. Surprisingly, she could feel sleep begin to creep up on her as he stroked her hair.

***

"Wake up, little one," he whispered in her ear. "It's time to rise and shine." She opened her eyes to see that it was already morning somehow.

"How did you do that?" she asked blearily. "The last thing I remember, you were rocking me."

"Daddy magic," he grinned, looking very proud of himself. "Now, get up and get dressed. I'll have breakfast waiting on you when you're done." She dragged herself reluctantly from under the covers and padded to the bathroom to get ready. True to his word, he had a full breakfast of pancakes and coffee waiting on the table.

"You look so beautiful, kitten," he said,

pulling out a chair for her to sit in. "Very professional." She had chosen a navy pantsuit and a plain white button-up, far more conservative than her usual shorts and swimsuits, and it felt strange.

"I'm not sure I can eat. I'm still really nervous."

"You'd better eat, young lady," he said firmly. "You're not going to that interview on an empty stomach, not on my watch. I'll feed you again if I have to." She giggled and threw her hands up in mock surrender.

"Alright, alright," she said. "I'll eat." After the first bite, she realized how ravenous she was and wolfed the rest of it down, gulping her coffee between bites. Within minutes, she had completely cleaned her plate. He insisted on driving her to her interview, saying that he wanted to be there when she got the good news. She smiled at his optimism, hoping that it was warranted. He held her hand the whole way there, and she was so grateful to have him by her side. No matter how the interview went, she at least had Paul. The interview was awkward at first, but as the conversation turned to the animals she would be caring for, her favorite subject in the whole world, she lit up. She felt more like herself, and the answers came easily. By the end of it, it felt like she and Mr. Chance were chatting like old friends. She did her best to keep her poker face on as she came out into the waiting room where Paul was waiting for her, wanting to keep him in suspense as he so often did to her.

"Well," he asked impatiently. "How did it go?" She broke out into a grin, unable to hold it back any longer.

"They want me to start next week," she said. He whooped with joy and wrapped his arms around her, swinging her around with unencumbered glee.

"See?" he laughed and kissed her on the lips. "I told you you'd get the job. Daddy is always right, remember that, little one." She laughed along with him, her heart overflowing with joy. She couldn't remember a time she had felt so at ease with someone before, certainly never someone who looked as handsome as Paul.

"I will. I promise, I've never had anyone believe in me as much as you do. Now, let's get out of here."

Chapter 15

They decided to spend the night at her place again.

"Wait right here," she said, as they came inside. She rushed off to her bedroom to find a silky nightgown, stripping off her suit and underwear. She pulled the black, lacy material down over her naked body. Wanting to make sure that she looked as good as possible, she ran her fingers through her hair, biting her lips slightly until they were pink and swollen and pinched her cheeks, a trick she had seen in an old movie. As she came back into the living room, the look on Paul's face was absolutely priceless as he stared at her in stunned silence.

"I know it's no diaper and t-shirt, but do you think this will do?" He nodded slowly, his wide eyes glued to the curves of her body. She crooked a finger at him, motioning for him to follow, then walked back to the bedroom. Behind her, she could hear the soft rustle of his shirt being pulled overhead followed by the quiet jingle of his pant being undone. She smiled quietly to herself at his eagerness. He caught up with her as they entered her room, his hands circling her waist and stopping her forward momentum. He touched her greedily, running his palms over the silky material of her negligee, relishing the warm softness of her flesh underneath. Her eyes fluttered closed, and she could feel the smile pulling at his lips as he brushed her long hair aside and kissed the curve where her neck and shoulder meet. Letting herself go, she freely moaned and writhed against him, stoking the fire. She pressed her backside against his growing erection, shivering as he bit her neck in response. The pain made her blood go hot, and he moaned as he sensed her heightened arousal, his breath moist and warm against her skin. He yanked the skirt of her negligee up, running his hands over the bare skin of her hips and stomach. She reached back and pulled him closer, leaning her head back on his chest as he enjoyed her body. His hands wandered upwards towards her breasts, cupping them gently and caressing her nipples lightly with his fingertips. The sensations took her breath away. The heady desire made her feel dizzy as he dug his fingernails into her tender skin. She gasped as the pain brought her sharply into the here and now, filling her with a frantic need. Impatient with lust, Amber lifted the negligee the rest of the way over her head and lie down on the bed, face down, hips lifted invitingly. He joined her, straddling her legs as he began to paint her back with delicate kisses. His cock was nestled between the warm soft flesh of her buttocks. Every small movement of her hips made him want to plunge himself inside of her, but he held back, sensing she was in the mood for a long, slow fuck. He lowered his weight onto her, gathering up her long hair so that he could access the curve of her neck. Working his way around with his tongue, he nipped the spot where her spine met her skull sending electric shivers throughout her entire being. Her back arched and she let out a deep guttural moan. He let his hands wander over the generous swell of her hips and buttocks. He shifted his legs to part hers and settled between them, seeking out the burning core of her desire. He ran his fingers lightly over her pubic hairs, tickling and teasing her sex, making her squirm pleasingly beneath her. His teasing fingers moved inward, teasing her folds and the hood of her clit, the light touch on her most sensitive parts driving her wild with need. She kicked her feet to expel some of the galvanizing energy dancing along her skin.

"Oh, we're just get started, my dear," he whispered, his breath hot against her ear.

"You're not going to get any relief for quite some time." Her agonized groan was music to his ears. She strained her hips backward, seeking more stimulation and he obliged, slipping a finger between her folds to discover the wetness pooling there.

"Oh my, you're a horny little thing, aren't you?" He circled her aching entrance, knowing just how much she longed to be filled, to be penetrated, but he wasn't ready to give her the satisfaction just yet. Instead, he smacked her ass firmly, watching it jiggle from the impact. He liked watching it so much, he did it again and again, until her pale flesh began to turn pink. Each impact stoked her passion all the more, her squeals and moans began to take on a pleading tone.

"What's wrong? Did you want my fingers inside of you again?" He stopped spanking her and went back to teasing her dripping slit.

"Yes, Daddy. Please!" she gasped out, already knowing it wouldn't be that easy.

"Unh-unh," he chimed in a sing-song tone. He traced a line of kisses down her spine, lifting her up by the hips and tilted her pelvis forward until he could bury his face in her fragrant pussy. His tongue explored and tasted her, deliberately avoiding the spots that gave her the most pleasure. He didn't let up until she was a quivering, dripping mess that could only emit a high-pitched whine, begging him me to fill her up, to fuck her hard, to use her over and over. Having finally gotten her to the desired level of desperation, he slowly slipped the tip of one finger into her, smiling to himself as she thrust her hips back, trying to take him deeper. He didn't give her more than his fingertip, however, no matter how she angled herself.

The lust and need had completely clouded her mind. All conscious thought had melted away leaving behind a mindless, rutting animal in heat, desperate to mounted. She was an aching void that needed to be filled, to be tamed, to be mastered. At last, she accepted his control over her pleasure, surrendering to the teasing torment of his fingertip. Feeling her give in, he rewarded her by plunging his finger inside of her, giving her the full penetration she needed so badly. With his free hand, he once again spanked her pink and tender bottom. As he worked his finger in and out of her, she got so lost in the steady rhythm of pain and pleasure that she edged dangerously close to an orgasm.

"Not yet, my pet," he whispered,

withdrawing his finger from her despite her greedy whimpers of protest. "Let's put that wet little mouth of yours to work, shall we?" He lie down on the bed, putting his hands behind his head so that he could better watch his sexy little fuck slave work her magic. Obediently, she got on all fours between his legs, then lowered herself down to her elbows with her ass up in the air like a playful puppy. Maintaining eye contact, she wrapped her lips around his swollen cock and swallowed him down her seemingly endless throat in one long, agonizingly slow motion. Once he was enveloped in her tight, warm throat entirely, she caressed his balls with her silky, cool fingertips. He almost came down her throat right then but just barely managed to hold himself back. She stilled herself until he regained his self-control, then began to face fuck herself with his cock, pushing past her own gag reflex to take his cock deeper and faster. He stroked her cheeks and hair as she serviced him, showing her how proud he was of her and how sexy she was to him. He watched her ass wiggle in the air as she bobbed her head up and down on his erection, slurping and moaning happily as she devoted herself entirely to his pleasure. Swallowing his cock made her feel strangely whole, as well as incredibly horny. Once again, she had to slow her pace so that he could retain his composure. Still too close to the edge, he pulled her off his dick by a fist full of hair, pulling her towards him until her perky breasts swung in his face. Capturing her nipple in his mouth, he sucked on it hard, delighting in the pain that shot through her and the way it made her grind her hot mound against his stomach. He scooted her hips down until his cock was resting against the cleft of her ass.

"Please, Daddy," she whined, rubbing her moist slit up the length of his hardness. "Please fuck me. I need to feel you inside of me." He spread her cheeks, teasing her entrance with the tip of his cock while he worked her nipple between her teeth. Slowly, he let himself slip inside of her, inching his way into her tight wetness. Her eyes rolled back as he, at last, filled her needy cunt. As he thrust into her, waves of pleasure came crashing down on her, and she was filled with the urgent need to cum.

"Daddy, please let me cum on your cock," she whined. He watched her riding him, looking so beautiful as her head rolled back, lost in ecstasy.

"Yes, princess. Cum on Daddy's cock like a good slut." She shuddered and twitched on top of him, lost in her own boundless universe of ecstasy. Her legs quivered and shook around him as she came, but he was far from satisfied with just one. He knew from experience that she had many more where that came from and he was going to fuck them all out of her. Her first orgasm left her all the more sensitive, so as he parted her thighs further so that he could penetrate her deeper, she could only throw her head back and try to hold on as he split her open. Gathering her wrists in his hands and forcing them behind her back, he battered her tender pussy, wanting to torture her with pleasure. He wrapped one hand around both of her delicate wrists and the other around her slender throat. As he squeezed, she relished the heady mixture of helplessness and trust that washed over her as she leaned into his hand, silently encouraging him to squeeze harder.

"Cum for me again, princess," he commanded, knowing that she was already getting close once more. She rode his cock in a slow and steady rhythm, her universe narrowed down to warm hardness stretching and filling her and his large, rough hands dominating her body. Another orgasm ripped through her, stronger than the first, his hardness thrusting into her with no mercy as she stiffened, her lips wordlessly moving. As her climax waned, he released her throat but not her hands.

Regaining her breath, she moaned loudly, her inhibitions totally melted away. She let herself surrender to the pounding between her legs, lost in an ocean of pleasure and submission. For his part, Paul was content to watch her bounce up and down on his cock. With her hands behind her back, it forced her chest forward, and her perfect tits bounced with every thrust. He reached up and grabbed a fistful of her hair, forcing her head back, exaggerating the effect even more.

"You are so fucking sexy. My sweet little fuckdoll. Mine. Mine. Mine." He slammed himself deep inside of her with every "mine." It felt so fucking good to be claimed by him, to feel like she belonged and that she was desirable. She couldn't get enough of fucking him, of cumming on his cock, of being his. He shifted on the small bed, gently guiding her to all fours as he knelt behind her. He took a moment to enjoy the view, her thighs and round ass parted slightly to reveal her glistening sex, slick with her orgasms. With a soft growl, he gave her a hard spank and entered her from behind. She dropped down to her elbows, allowing him to go deeper. As he gripped her hips and thrust into her, they were both soon lost in the ancient rhythm of grunts and thrust and moans. They existed outside of time, his desire stoking hers as hers did his, both with an endless hunger they never wanted to be sated. He grabbed her hand, guiding it to her clit.

"You're going to make Daddy cum, and I want you to cum with me, got that princess?

"Yes Daddy," she gasped, working her clit furiously as he pounded into her. Once again, he grabbed a fistful of her hair, forcing her head back. The pain sent her over the edge, and she screamed as she came. As her pussy pulsed around him, he couldn't hold on any longer and released himself inside of her. As he lay on the mattress, beside her, he found her hand and brought it to his lips for a kiss. She snuggled close to him, laying her head on his chest and listened to his pounding heart.

Chapter 16

Finally, graduation day arrived. She Skyped with her Mom who was unable to get away from work and unable to afford the ticket from the mainland anyway. Hannah was happy just to see her face and hear her voice. It had been quite some time since they had seen each other.

"I can't believe my baby is graduating with honors," her mom cried. "You've worked so hard for so long. I'm so proud of you." She introduced Paul to her Mom while she had her on video chat. Even though they had technically only been together for a very short period of time, she knew that this was the man for her, and she wanted the whole world to know it. Her mother seemed thoroughly charmed by him, almost as charmed as Hannah was. The graduation ceremony was short and sweet. It wasn't a very large school, so Hannah was only one of a few students getting their diplomas that day. Afterward, she was taking a few celebratory selfies with her classmates when she saw Paul carrying a bouquet of flowers and a gift bag, scanning the crowd for her. She waved him down and crossed the crowd to meet him. Paul handed her the flowers, and she blushed, sniffing them discreetly.

"I got you another graduation present," he said, holding up the gift bag. "But, you might want to open this one in private." She blushed even deeper and looked around her shyly, wondering what it could be.

"Just let me know when you're done here, and I'll take you back to my place." She slid her hand into his, ready to follow him anywhere.

"I'm ready now," she said. "Let's go."

***

Back at his place, she opened his other present eagerly. Inside was a small velvet box, like a jewelry box. Inside was a silver pacifier with "Daddy's Girl" engraved into it. She examined it more closely to find that it was a fully functioning pacifier, complete with a rubber tip.

"Oh Daddy, I love it," she exclaimed, slipping it in her mouth to try it out.

"I'm so glad," he said. "I wanted to give you something that showed you how much you mean to me. I'm so grateful to have you in my life. I know that we've only been together a short time but, Hannah, I love you." She stared at him in shock as the words sank in. Her jaw went so slack that the pacifier fell right out and into her lap.

"You make me so happy, baby girl,' he continued. "Happier than I've ever been before, happier than I ever could have dreamed. You're all I've ever wanted. I used to dream about what it would be like to have someone to come home to, someone to protect and look after. Now that I have you, it's better than I ever could have imagined it. You don't have to say it back if it's too early -"

"I love you too," she said quietly,

interrupting him. He smiled at her in happy relief.

"You do? Oh pumpkin, that's fantastic."

"Of course I do. I'm absolutely crazy about you, Paul." He kissed her softly on the lips and pulled her close against him. Very quickly, their kisses grew more heated, and they fell back onto the couch. He moaned into her mouth as their tongues meet, grinding his already hard cock against her needy sex. He pulled the straps of her dress down and captured her nipple with his teeth, teasing her and watching her writhe beneath him. He squeezed her breasts together and buried his face in her cleavage, licking and nibbling hungrily. She suddenly ached to feel his skin against her and pulled at his shirt, whining with impatience as he pulled it over his head. As he settled back on top of her, she ran her hands over the muscles of his back. Their naked flesh pressed together as he kissed her again. He lifted up the skirt of her dress and growled with approval when he sees that she's not wearing any panties, a little surprise just for him.

"So naughty, little one," he said with a grin and lowered himself between her legs. With a deep breath in to savor her scent, he teased her lightly with his tongue. She gripped her thighs, holding her legs wide open as he continued to explore her dripping folds. He moaned as he tasted her, working his way inward, seeking out her clit. She whimpered as he twirled his tongue around her sensitive spot, her legs began to quiver as he picked up speed. He sank a finger into her tight pussy, watching how it made her squirm, then a second finger, stretching her out as she gasped and moaned. His fingers pumped in and out of her as his tongue traced circles of ecstasy over her clit. She already felt a powerful orgasm building, but she held off, waiting for his permission like a good girl. Finally, he stopped pleasuring her long enough to pull her dress the rest of the way off. He pulled the rest of his clothes off as well, freeing his rock hard cock. She stared at it longingly, watching it as he stroked it seductively, her expression get hungrier by the minute.

"Turn over, princess," he said. "Get that sexy ass in the air." His voice was gruff and commanding, making her body thrill with arousal. Eagerly, she rolled onto her tummy, sticking her ass straight up just as he instructed. She waited like that as he looked at her for a long while and continued to pleasure himself. Her pussy was throbbing, but she waited obediently for what would come next. As always, the anticipation only heightened her desire for him. He smacked her ass hard enough to make her pussy tingle. She moaned as he spanked her again and again until her cheeks burned. Once he was satisfied with how pink her ass cheeks had gotten, he grabbed her by the hair and brought her mouth to his cock. She opened for him eagerly as he thrust himself deep into her throat.

"That's it, baby," he moaned. "Suck it down deep like a good slut. Oh fuck, you're such a talented cocksucker." She moaned around his cock, loving the dirty way he talked to her when they fucked. He plunged his cock deeper, making her choke and drool. Every thrust down her throat made the ache in her pussy grow. The rougher he used her, the wilder it made her feel. He pulled out of her throat with a satisfied sigh and sat on the couch. He pulled her onto his lap so that she was straddling him. He bit down hard on her nipple, snickering at the way it made her writhe against him.

"Play with that needy pussy, baby," he muttered, pulling her cheeks apart before giving them a firm slap. "Show Daddy how badly you need this cock." She rubbed her clit frantically and ground her labia against his cock, so tantalizingly close to being inside of her. Even though he hadn't yet given her permission to cum, she felt herself getting dangerously close. He could tell from her frenzied moans that she was riding the line and grabbed a fistful of her hair to remind her of her place.

"Easy, little one," he growled. "If you cum without permission, I won't let you cum again for a whole week, understood?" She whimpered softly but slowed her pace.

"I understand, Daddy."

"Good girl." He pushed his cock toward her slick entrance, making her gasp with need.

"Who does this pussy belong to?"

"This pussy belongs to you," she cried out. He impaled her with his cock as a reward, making her eyes roll back as he buried himself inside of her in one swift thrust.

"That's right," he whispered. "Don't you fucking forget it, my precious little slut." Her back arched as he pounded into her, still playing with her clit. She moved hips to meet his, sliding up and down the length of him. She was on the edge of cumming on his cock as she rode him, gritting her teeth as she fought to stay in control.

"Mmm, my baby girl needs it badly, doesn't she?"

"Yes, Daddy! I need to cum so bad. Please, please, please ..." The words trailed off. She was so enraptured by lust that the words seemed to fail her. He laughed at her and twisted her nipples hard, making her gasp.

"Oh, I know you can do better than that, pumpkin. Beg like a good little, and Daddy might let you cum." She whimpered and slow down her pace, trying her best to focus. His cock was so distracting, though, and the pain in her nipples certainly didn't help.

"Please, Daddy. I want to cum on your cock so bad. I've been a good girl. Please let me cum. Your cock feels so good inside my slutty little pussy. Please, Daddy, can I?"

"Much better," he growled. He gripped her by the hips and flipped her onto her back, spreading her legs wide open as he rammed into her, hard and swift. "You can cum whenever you like, baby girl." He slammed into her, deep and furious. She rubbed her clit and wrapped her thighs around him, holding on tightly as her orgasm erupted. His head snapped back as the ecstasy to her, and she moaned with abandon. He had turned her into quite the screamer, she noted.

"That's right, sweetie, cum for Daddy. Just

like that. That's a good girl." He kissed her sweaty neck, and she tremble underneath him as he continued to fuck her. Shivers of pleasure ran through her even after the main wave passed. His thrusts did not slow in the least. He kept pounding into her, growling as he became wrapped up in his own pleasure.

"Oh, darling. You get so wet when you cum, did you know that? Such a sweet, dirty girl. You make Daddy's cock feel so good." She absolutely loved how vocal he got when he got close to cumming. She loved being reassured that she was his fantasy, his perfect girl. His muscles clenched. She knew that he was close, that her reward was coming any second now.

"Fuck yeah, baby girl. Keep taking Daddy's cock just like that. Oh, you're such a good girl. Daddy's good little slut. Here it comes, baby!" His body seized up, except for his cock, which pumped her full with his hot cum. With a groan, he collapsed against her, burying his head into her cleavage. He held her close to him, still inside of her, until he regained his breath. She kissed his sweaty forehead as she held him, a feeling of complete contentment washing over her. It seemed like a small miracle that they had found each other, that they completed one another so perfectly. She squeezed him tighter, hoping that she would be able to hold him like this forever.

Chapter 17

Three months later, Hannah awoke in her own bed with Paul sprawled out on the bed beside her, naked and snoring softly. She felt a wave of affection for him as she watched him sleep. As the next months rolled by, things between them only seemed to get better and better. They spent nearly every night together, and she had yet to grow tired of him, and she suspected that she never would. It was sort of an unwritten rule that whoever woke up first would wake the other one up with a little oral pleasure. It looked this morning. The privilege would be hers. As quietly as she could, she pulled the covers back and lowered herself until her face was level to his cock. Even soft, it was impressive to look at, laying across his toned belly, just waiting to spring to life. Slowly, she took the head into her mouth, gently applying pressure as she ran her tongue over the sensitive tip. He made a soft noise but didn't open his eyes just yet.

As she took him further into her mouth, she could feel his cock begin to stiffen as the blood flooded in. He still tasted of their shared juices from the night before, and she moaned lightly as she tasted him. He had gotten her addicted to the taste of her own pussy, associating it with the toe-curling pleasure he always gave her. As he grew harder, she began to apply more pressure, delighting in how responsive he was. His reactions made him a delight to pleasure. With a happy sigh, he finally opened his eyes and looked down at her with sleepy affection. He smiled and ran his fingers lightly through her hair as she worked his cock deeper into her throat.

"Good morning. Didn't get enough last night, huh little one?" he purred. "Mmm, I love how greedy you are for my cock." Grabbing a handful of her hair, he pushed her down further onto him, his partially erect member sliding easily down her throat. It was delightful, feeling a fullness in her throat without feeling like she had to gag, and she swallowed him greedily. He stroked her face as she pleasured him, getting harder and harder.

"Oh fuck, kitten!" Paul threw his head back against the pillow. "That's so good. Suck Daddy's cock." Hannah's body tingled with desire as she gagged and choked on him. She sucked him harder and faster, wanting to taste his cum, her favorite treat.

"Hold on, baby girl," he suddenly growled, pulling her up. She nearly whined with disappointment, but he cut it short by pulling her up for a deep kiss, fisting his hands into her hair. She straddled him and melted against him as his greedy tongue pushed into her mouth, his teeth lightly grazing her lip. "I'm not ready to cum just yet."

He pulled her hair and tugged her head to the side, exposing her neck. He held her like that as he kissed and bit her neck, making her squirm with desire. He knew just how to get her horny and desperate for him and did so as often as possible.

She gripped his broad shoulders as he devoured her neck, moaning softly as the mild pain in her scalp only intensified her need, craving more. She felt helpless pinned against him like that, and that helplessness was exhilarating. There was a tremendous amount of freedom in that helplessness for her, freedom to be as nasty as he wanted her to be. With his free hand, he dug his fingers into the flesh of her ass as he pulled her closer against his throbbing member. With a vicious growl, he brought his hand down sharply onto her ass, spanking her forcefully. She moaned loudly as he brought his hand down, again and again, keeping her pinned against him with his fist in her hair. The flesh of her buttocks stung more and more with every blow, and she could feel her pussy responding with an aching need, but she knew he wouldn't stop until her ass was bright red. She squirming against him as he spanked her, inching him closer and closer to her entrance, desperate to have him inside of her. He growled in her ear, bringing his hand even harder down onto her buttocks, knowing full well that it only made her want him all the more.

"You're so impatient, little one," he teased. "You just can't wait for Daddy to fuck you can you?" She whined and writhed against him, but he only spanked her again. His blows beginning to come harder and harder as he masterfully teased her, inflaming her desire.

"Tell Daddy what you want," he said. He loved to make her say the filthiest things, loved the way it only made her pussy wetter when she let herself be the depraved slut she tried to keep hidden away from the rest of the word. She knew that he would not give her what she so desperately needed until she asked for it, possibly even begged for it. She had gotten pretty good at begging these past few months, if she did say so herself.

"I want your cock, Daddy," she whined. "I want you to fuck me so hard that it hurts. Please give me your big fat cock, Daddy." Suddenly, he shifted her weight, flipping her onto her back and kneeling between her knees, pushing her legs wide open. She gasped loudly as he began to run the tip of his cock over her clit, rubbing it in slow circles. Nothing made him happier than torturing her with pleasure.

"Do you want Daddy's cock, is that it little one?" he said with a husky voice. She stared down, fascinated by the sight of his cock gliding over her, and nodded. "I didn't hear you that time, sweetie."

"Yes, I want your cock, Daddy. Please, I need it so bad, please fuck me!" With a satisfied sneer, he plunged into her, roaring with satisfaction as he buried himself inside of her to the hilt. Hannah made a roar of her own, grasping his buttocks to pull him closer. Her entire body felt alive as he stretched her open, taking her hard and fast. He unleashed his passion onto her, rutting into her like a crazed animal. His hands twisted into her hair, yanking her hair back as he drove himself into her furiously.

"Is that what you wanted, kitten?" he growled into her ear.

"Yes, Daddy. I love it when you fuck me

hard!" As his thick cock split her open again and again, she could feel a climax building. She raked her nails over his back and buttocks, wild with pleasure.

"Good girl," he laughed playfully. "Are you ready to cum for Daddy, princess?" He reached down and began to stroke her clit with his thumb as he pounded into her, overwhelming her with ecstasy. The double stimulation was too much for her, and she thrashed her head from side to side. If he didn't either stop or give her permission soon, she would totally lose control.

"Yes, Daddy. Can I please?" The effort of holding herself back made the words came out strangled.

"Yes, little one," he said, rubbing her clit even faster. "Cum for Daddy." Within seconds, another orgasm broke over her, stronger than the first. She let herself go completely, trembling and moaning beneath him.

"Oh fuck, baby girl, you're so tight around my cock." As Hannah's quaking orgasm began to recede, his thrusts quickened. She could feel his manhood grow even harder inside of her, throbbing on the edge of release. "Look at me." He loved maintaining eye contact as they fucked, loved to keep her attention focused solely on him. He yanked her hair harder to bring her face closer to his, holding her face firmly with his other hand. The possessive way his fingers dug into her face always gave her a sense of belonging.

"You're mine," he said, holding her gaze with his chocolate brown eyes. "Aren't you, slut? My slut." She never got tired of hearing it or saying it. She was his, and he was hers forever.

"I'm yours, Daddy," she whispered. He pulled her face to his for a kiss, deep but tender.

"Yes," he whispered, his breath hot against her lips. "All mine." His rhythm suddenly faltered, and she could feel his grip on her hair tightening as his body went rigid. His cock throbbed and twitched inside of her as he filled her up with his seed. With one final shudder, he collapsed against her and buried his face in her neck, his breath ragged. They didn't have the luxury of lingering in bed, however. Their morning sex usually didn't leave much time for breakfast, but it was well worth it in Hannah's mind. Even with the time crunch, he took the time to diaper her lovingly. She loved wearing her diaper all day at work. Not only did it provide her with a source of comfort when things got hectic, it also reminded her of Paul and what a truly wonderful Daddy he was to her. She loved being his little. They ate a quick breakfast together in contented silence, sipping coffee and reading the newspaper or their phones. Hannah treasured these quiet moments together before the hubbub of the day began. She loved her job and would be eternally grateful to Paul for helping her to land it, but it had its challenges and stresses just like any job. That hubbub began all too soon as she dumped her plate and cup in the sink and ran upstairs to get dressed. She mostly interacted with turtles and penguins all day, so she never wasted too much time on her hair and makeup. Most days, she just threw on some khaki shorts and the aquarium uniform and put her hair up in a ponytail.

"You look beautiful, baby girl," Paul said as she came back downstairs. He always said that, no matter how she looked, never letting her forget that she was his dream woman. She had expected his constant praise of her beauty to fade with time, but it hadn't. He still looked at her the same way as when they had first started dating. He was already dressed and had a travel mug of coffee for each of them ready to go.

"I love you so much, sweet girl," he said, kissing her sweetly and deeply. Even three months later, it always took her breath away, and she never got tired of hearing it.

"I love you too, Paul," she said. "I'll miss you today." As he kissed her again, she thought about their tentative discussions about consolidating their lives. Even though nothing had been decided yet, it felt to her more of a question of when rather than if. There would be a ton of details to work out such as who would move where, but it just made sense to simplify their lives by moving in together. They spent all of their time together anyway, so why not move in together? It just made sense. The two of them freely admitted that this was the happiest they had ever been. They both had jobs they loved nearby, and they fit together so well, supporting and loving each other unconditionally. Even when he had to go out of town for a work trip, she could usually get off of work from her own job to go with him. They rarely fought, facing any problem with honest, open communication. Hannah was never one to let bottled up feelings and mixed signals to ever threaten their happiness, and it turned out that Paul was the same way. As a result, this had been the healthiest and happiest relationship of her life, and she was determined to make it work for the long haul. Paul handed her a travel mug of coffee of her own, still groggily wiping the sleep from his eyes. He was not a morning person which made him getting up early enough to drive her to work all the more romantic.

"Are you ready to go, princess?" he asked, kissing her once more, this time on the forehead. Even though her car had been working just fine ever since they got it back from the mechanic, he still insisted on driving her to work and picking her up whenever their schedules allowed. He said it allowed them to spend more time together, something they always wanted more of. She was happy to oblige, happy to let him spoil and pamper her all he wanted. She freely admitted that he had spoiled her rotten as if either of them would have it any other way. No one else could ever come close to comparing with her Daddy.

"Yeah, I'm ready," she said. "Let's go." He kissed her softly, his lips lingering over hers, and sighed contentedly as he stared down at her with a quizzical expression on his face.

"Are you happy, my darling?" he asked. She grinned, certain that the answer was written all over her face.

"Completely."

Who is Tina Moore?

Tina Moore has enjoyed the lifestyle of a Mommy Domme for several years. She began exploring kink and BDSM in her youth and found her love of being a strict Mommy Domme in early 2000. Tina Moore is now an author of many MDLG, DDLG and ABDL themed novels.

Follow her on:

Author Page on Amazon

Instagram @tinamoore.kdp